A World Colored Blue

Jillian Rose Sherwin

ISBN:9781677777686

ACKNOWLEDGMENTS

When I was younger, I imagined writers as people who sat in their dark, dusty attics all by themselves, writing on a typewriter and crumpling up the pages they didn't like. It wasn't until I started writing this book that I realized I had a lot of misconceptions about being a writer. When I wrote this book, I didn't use a typewriter, didn't sit in attics, and definitely didn't work alone (but I did crumple pages!). This book would not have been possible without a group of people who supported me through the writing process, and who I would like to take the time to thank.

First off, I want to acknowledge my good friend Brenna Hamlin who gave me the initial prompt for this book and sat by me day after day while I wrote. As soon as I finished a chapter she would read through it and offer amazing feedback. When I was stuck she always helped me talk through plot points, and together we got inside the characters' heads to really understand what they were going through. She picked up on all the secret clues in my book, and it is amazing to have such a supportive friend who is as in love with this book as I am. Thank you Brenna for the crazy prompt, the laughs, and helping talk me down from bad book endings. You have been there through this whole process and I have no words to express how thankful I am.

Next I want to thank my teachers, Hannah Levinger and Spike Carter for all their support. Not only did they read my book but they gave me endless tips on how to continue writing through my rough stages. Spike: thank you for reading my prologue when I first wrote it and pushing me to make this book a real novel! You were my motivator to get past 40,000 words. Having your support and enthusiasm through this whole process has meant so much to me. Hannah: thank you for introducing me to my inner critic and teaching me how to tell her to go sit in the corner! Also, thank you for all those times I sent you emails with grammar questions. This book would be a mess without you.

Publishing this book would not have been possible without the amazing book cover designed and created by Meadow McGalliard. Meadow, thank you so much for making it with me and putting up with my constant edits.

In addition to the outside of the book, the inside of the book was a process as well. I want to thank Leland Pelletier who helped me through all my formatting problems and always made sure to remind me that it was going to look great and everything was going to be okay. Thanks for always supporting me through the ups and downs.

I also want to thank the group of Rocharons who allowed me to use their personalities and appearances as characters in the book. I hope when you read this you all see how much I love you and our little community.

I want to appreciate my mother, the Rochester community, and The Sharon Academy who all supported my writing. Thank you to each and everyone who added and liked my Facebook and Instagram pages and shared in my excitement as the publishing process happened. Last but not least I want to say thank you to everyone who read part or all of my book while I was writing and gave me feedback; Brenna, Olivia, Finley, Eve, Leland, Anika, Abby, Izzy, and Hannah's creative writing elective 2019. This book would not have been possible without each and every one of these people and so many more not listed here.

If you're reading this, thank you for taking the time to buy and read these words that I've typed on the page. You have no idea how much it means to me.

AUTHORS NOTE

When I wrote this book I fell in love with the name Chaeronea. In my mind it was a beautiful way to spell Sharona. However, it wasn't until I wrote the book that I realized Chaeronea is the name of a Greek town and it is not pronounced the same way as Sharona. I thought about changing the name to Sharona or even Cherona, but I really couldn't part with the spelling of Chaeronea. As you read this book, please pretend that Chaeroneas mother decided to go with an untraditional spelling Sharona.

PROLOGUE

This had never happened to her before.

But had it ever happened to anyone before?

She wore a shockingly red dress that reached her knees with a high neckline and no sleeves. The material was that of a party dress, stiff but flowy, not made for comfort but for looks. She sat in the middle of the church aisle, head on her knees, feet together, arms wrapped around her shins; a child's comfort position. She didn't speak, she didn't move; she tried to breathe.

After several long moments of stunning silence, she lifted her head. Quiet tears streamed down her face, but she didn't even know she was crying. Still in shock, her green eyes scanned the ruins around her. She took in a fallen rafter on the altar, a shattered ceiling fan on the dark wood floor, and the clock that lay in front of her feet. Surprisingly, it was still ticking, mockingly reminding her that this was reality. Barely able to make out the shapes of the world around her through her tears, she scanned the white pews that always hurt her back as she sat in them. They were scattered with debris. She silently noted millions of small red flower petals and white fuzzy bulbs scattered on the burgundy carpet.

Red. The color of the flowers, of the dresses. The color her sister had chosen; the color of blood.

It was all too much, and slowly, she closed her eyes, lying down on the floor. First placing her head down on the hardwood, and then sliding her feet until the back of her legs reached the floor. She could feel glass beneath her, but she didn't care. She tried to make sense of the moments that had happened so fast.

She remembered the sound of the giant glass windows breaking, the panes exploding like fireworks, the shards falling like confetti; sharp confetti that had landed on her skin like icy needles.

Her hair had fallen out of it's perfectly made bun, soft brown curls falling out as she frantically turned her head and watched the panic just as everyone turned to see what noise had just interrupted the ceremony. The congregants became blurs of purples, blues, and greens as they rushed to the doorway; long sweeps of fabric ruffling around knees, as if they had a mind of their own. It was almost fall, and the leaves had started to turn beautiful shades of red, yellow, and orange. The temperature had started to drop in the evenings, causing everyone to start pulling out their long sleeved clothing from dusty boxes in their attics. But today, for the special occasion, everyone had worn their bright colored clothing before they had to be put away for the winter.

She remembered the look on her sister's face. The way the roof fell down around her, and how everyone seemed to stop breathing at the same time. She lay on the floor thinking, wishing. Wishing it didn't happen and wishing she could stop thinking.

Thinking about why she had to wish in the first place.

When a day is ruined, is it just a disappointment? Or can it be more, can it be a tragedy? What qualifies as a tragedy? How many people have to die? How many times does a little girl have to scream? Her mind could only focus on the present, not bothering to wonder what would happen next, or how it had happened in the first place. It was almost as if her brain was a CD repeating the same song; she silently screamed, pleading it to turn it off, but she couldn't reach the button.

She was useless. She was laying on the floor, useless. What could she do? What did she know that could help her right now?

They don't teach these kinds of things in school.

And when she opened her eyes, she saw the afternoon sky where the roof should have been. A beautiful photograph, jagged at the edges by the zigzagged lines of the church walls. Above her, everything was dark and angry, thick clouds threatening to rain.

Her sister had been so worried about the rain ruining her day. She had even made her mom go and buy umbrellas for everyone just in case. Those umbrellas were neatly put in a pot near the front entrance. She turned her head to see them, still perfectly in place, untouched by the chaos that surrounded it.

On his jacket, her sister's fiance's military badges had lost their usual impressive shine, and were replaced by a dullness that consumed the whole atmosphere.

Her great-grandmother's vale was ripped down the middle, lying at the bottom of the altar; an heirloom that had meant so much to the family.

Now, it didn't matter.

Nothing mattered.

And all she could think about, was why her sister had chosen to have her wedding on the day the world ended.

○○○

The Code of Classification:

Classification is the universal way to keep peace.

Everyone is satisfied when each person knows who they truly are and how they fit into the world around them, which is why classification is necessary.

Domination is how we control the classification and keep peace over the land. Dominance is something to stay proud of, and it is a community members job to stay firm in our one and only belief that this is the way to keep the world safe.

Any persons involved with an act of declassification will be charged with treason, for it is in the best interest of all people of The House to live together harmoniously in classification. Therefore, any way that a person can make a community un-harmonious is considered an act of declassification.

By eliminating perspective, we lead the world into an unchangeable state of happiness because we can all see things the right way. We are classified as people who agree unequivocally.

Questioning is an outdated word in times like these, for when we all live harmoniously, un-chaotically, there is no need to throw around ideas of other possibilities, classification works, and it is all how it should be.

Part One

"The course of true love never did run smooth."
William Shakespeare, *A Midsummer's Night Dream*
I.i.134

CHAPTER ONE

"You want me to drink *this?*" Liam asked her, his blue eyes opened wide, holding out the large blue mug before him. Sylvia hoisted herself onto the black and white speckled countertop while laughing at him. She knew from the minute she started making the tea that he wouldn't want to drink it. Liam looked at her in disbelief, then back at the mug, twirling the orange liquid inside. He wore a light blue long sleeve with blue jeans, a piece of his black hair fell on his forehead.

"It will help your back," Sylvia said through laughter, only to receive another look of disbelief from Liam. "Seriously! Just try, it tastes like green tea with cinnamon." She pushed her own long brown hair behind her right ear. She also wore a long sleeve shirt with a red flannel over it, and she pulled the cuffs of the soft flannel around her hands, even though it wasn't cold.

"Odd combination," He observed, "but you're the expert." He raised the tea closer to his mouth and raised an eyebrow before sipping it, and after deciding that it did in fact taste good, he began to drink more. He watched her fiddle with the rings on her fingers, something she didn't even know she did.

Liam finished his tea and went to wash his mug in the old dented sink at the bottom of the staircase. The metal sink creaked and leaked as Liam turned it on to rinse his mug, but they loved the pre-Awakening artifact non the less.

Sylvia watched Liam for a moment before getting off the countertop and walking around to the other side, pulling a white packet of papers closer to her and leaning her elbows down beside it. She tucked her hair behind her ear, grabbed a pencil and scanned the first page. The top of the paper read: Community Census 2021

She sighed and felt Liam's slightly damp hands on her waist and his chin on her shoulder. He eyed the paper, "Census come out?" He hummed.

Sylvia flipped a page, "Yeah" she sighed "help me fill it out, I have no idea what I put last year."

"Okay," Liam started, "Just start with something simple like," He paused, scanning the questions, "favorite color."

He smirked as Sylvia groaned, rolling her eyes and leaning her head back against him. "I hate choosing a favorite."

"I know" Liam chuckled, kissing her on the cheek, "Just remember, it has to be the same one as last year." He said robotically.

"That's why I hate this. I understand we need to be classified. And they supposedly need to know these things, but why can't we change every year? People grow, people adapt, and people find different colors appealing every year. I don't mind being classified as a red lover as long as I can change it to blue if I want to next year." Sylvia sighed.

Liam readjusted his grip around her waist as she wrapped her own arms around her body. "But the only reason people change is because they grow into something better V, and The House wants everyone to believe they are the best versions of themselves under classification. There's no need to change if you're perfect, and if you know exactly who you are."

"Whose side are you on?" She laughed.

"Yours, always, just don't want you to be classified as one of those rabble rousers." He winked.

"You and your fancy words." She smirked.

"Right back at you," he said, turning her around in his arms, "And by the way, you put blue down last year because you thought it would be easiest to remember, considering it's your last name." Sylvia's eyes shone with realization and she quickly turned to mark that on the page before Liam turned her around.

"I love you." He murmured, centimeters apart.

"Right back at you," She smirked before turning back around to the packet. "C'mon we still have all these questions and it's due before Karma Day." She sighed.

Liam walked around to the other side of the counter, leaning down and turning the paper around for him to see. "Yeah, how are you feeling about that anyway?" He asked, looking up at her.

Sylvia met his gaze, "Karma Day?" She questioned, meeting his gaze and pushing the paper aside, shrugging, "I mean, I guess a little nervous, for Matilda and everything." Sylvia trailed off, "It's just, Karma Day." She added, pushing her hair behind her ear

Liam sensed her worry, "It's also Tuesday." He blurted out. Where had that come from? He had no idea. But when her eyes brightened around the edges all he knew was that it was worth it. He walked around the counter and pulled her into a hug, letting that say everything he was trying to.

"I'm worried about her too, but she's a strong kid. She's gonna do fine. And, I'm right here with you" He said into her ear, getting quieter as he spoke until it was almost a whisper. He leaned in to kiss her, slowly, comforting, and when they pulled away, Sylvia opened her mouth to speak but instead of words, bells rang from outside. Her open mouth closed into a smile.

"I think you should get to work." Sylvia brought her hand to the curl that dangled over his forehead and tried to push it out of his face.

He ran a hand through his short black hair after her, "Yes, yeah, I guess you're probably right." He pulled on his navy jacket and shouldered his dark messenger bag, moving towards the wooden door. Hand on the gray metal knob he turned to face Sylvia who had followed behind him.

"Hey, be careful while I'm gone, okay?" He said, turning around, not wanting to leave the comfort of her presence to the outside world. He dared to look into her green eyes, knowing that after all this time she wasn't going to take the question as a failure or fault in character, but instead as a genuine worry. A question he needed answered for his own peace of mind. Especially in the world they lived in.

She smiled at the question he asked everyday and responded. "You know me." She laughed, "I'll be fine," she reassured. And her eyes never left his blue ones, "Now get going, don't want to be late."

He believed her, and with his lopsided grin he left, the bell on the door jingling as it closed.

Sylvia, alone in her shop, turned her hand-painted sign to "Open". She lifted the curtains of the store windows, letting in the golden tint of morning sun. It flooded the room, the rays falling on the light wooden floor. Then she turned to take in her shop. The left and back walls were filled with jars of different shapes and sizes, colors and textures. All coming together into a smell that couldn't quite be described. *Dreams*, Liam had once said, *If dreams had a smell, it would be this shop.*

To her left was a small couch and armchair, both in green upholstery with yellow pillows and fringe, and as she walked by she adjusted the throw blanket on the couch. A bookshelf crammed with hardcover stories stood near that, Sylvia loved books, always had, and she ran her finger across the spines. And of course there was a small table in the sitting area. A brown wooden one, the only remaining item of her life before the Awakening. A table, stained with the dark color of coffee and a faint haze of her mother's perfume. At least, she thought she could still smell it. The place where her family had sat to play poker and other card games. The surface where cheese and drinks would sit on a Sunday afternoon. The table she would leave her book when her father carried her up the stairs, asleep in his arms.

She had found the table on a street sale during the Beginning, and recognizing it easily, had traded seven rations of her chocolate for it. Storing it in random places until she graduated.

The left side of her shop held a counter, and behind the wall of spices, a staircase adorned with a blue rug. Above the shop was the apartment she shared with Liam. At the foot of the stairs the sink lived, an unusual spot for such a well used appliance.

Plants hung all over her shop. Spices and herbs that grow in hanging pots and bowls, whatever she could find. Their vines and stems and stalks grew over the edges of the bowls, slowly creeping down and curling around themselves.

She loved her spice shop, it wasn't her original plan, but she still loved it. All her life she had wanted to be a doctor. She had wanted to help people, during the Khaos. During her schooling, when the ruling Powers had gotten rid of doctors, she had settled for the next best thing; a herbalist. As long as she was registered as a spice shop owner no one would question her, and the people of the community didn't mind her. They liked her in fact, they felt safe knowing they had someone at least close to a doctor in their midst.

Sylvia hung the dry mugs from the day before on the mug rack and went to sit behind the counter. While she waited for her first customer she spent time filling out the census. She started by writing out her last name in the vertical spaces provided, and then writing out what each letter stood for.

Beginning.

Linguistics.

Undertaker.

E*veryone is satisfied when each person knows who they truly are and how they fit into the world around them, which is why classification is necessary.*

That's what Sylvia's last name meant. Everyone had a four letter last name, unless you were of great importance in the scheme of things.

The first letter accounted for when you joined The House. K stood for Khaos, also known as the Before. They were the ones who were born into the system, the ones whose parents were involved even before the Awakening. B was for Beginning. Those were the ones who joined during the two years of the Awakening, also known as During. These people were known to have the worst and most tragic histories, not that any of them talked about it. If you joined during the Beginning it meant that your family was most likely killed in the Awakening, and you had nowhere else to go. W stood for the Witness times, everywhere from the end of the Awakening to now. Liam had joined right in the beginning of the Witness times, a mere two months after the Awakening. That's when they had met.

The second letter of your last name was your best class in school. Sylvia's had always been Linguistics. She could speak five languages, even though it was only required to be fluent in two. The Reining Powers didn't care *what* language you spoke, just that everyone agreed communication was necessary. Liam could speak three and a half languages, so she liked being able to communicate with him in different ways.

The third letter was your job, determined when you were 5. If you joined The House when you were older it was decided then. Classification was key, no one wanted to interrupt the processes. No one wanted to shift the fundamentals of The House. Sylvia's letter was U, Undertaker. The undertakers were the ones who ran businesses around the community; shops and restaurants.

The fourth letter was one of the mottos of The House that your teachers wanted you to remember. Something you had struggled with, or something that reminded you of your place. Sylvia's motto was, *Everyone is satisfied when each person knows who they truly are and how they fit into the world around them, which is why classification is necessary*. It was given to her after the mandatory interview everyone gets when they join The House. Sylvia was asking too many questions, instead of the interviewer asking them to her.

She was snapped out of her thoughts by a man coming into her shop. He had white hair and black glasses on. He was tall and lean, his arms swinging near his sides. His presence filled the room, and to most he would be intimidating. But to Sylvia, he was just another customer. She stood tall, no one intimidated her. His appearance seemed familiar to her, although she knew she had never seen him before.

"Hello, can I help you find something in particular?" She asked with a bright smile.

The man took some time with his answers, as if he was fighting between wanting to say one thing and knowing he should say another. His eyes grazed over the jars of spices. Sylvia noticed the way his fingers tapped against his legs, she noticed how his strides were firm and with purpose. She realized that even with all the confidence that surrounded him, right here right now, he felt awkward; out of place in a new environment, and she wondered where he had come from.

"I have teas and spices for flavoring, I have sweets and fresh herbs. But if you're looking for something else, there's a lot of books over on the bookshelf. I also make an excellent conversationalist if you're looking for one." She smiled with confidence, even with an anxious note from earlier. She observed how slowly he turned to face her, as though he was fearful she would recognize him. Observation, that was one of Sylvia's best skills. Observing, and getting to know you better than you know yourself. She noticed how some people pulled on their ears, how others always started a sentence with the same word. These skills helped make her almost psychic; if she knew you well enough she would be able to predict your next word, movement, or thought.

Sometimes, Liam found it creepy. In that, 'Wow, you are good,' kind of way.

"I'm- I'm just looking for some peppermint sticks. I've run out at my house." The man finally spoke, putting his hands in his pockets and shrugging. He opened a can that was sitting on the countertop and smelled the contents, lemongrass.

"I have those right here." And she wrapped two sticks up in wax paper, setting them into the man's hand. She rang him up, and watched as his eyes flirted around the room, curious of his surroundings. When he left, Sylvia made sure she would remember it all and tell Liam when he got home.

Sylvia didn't have to wait long for her next customer. About twenty minutes later, a younger man walked into the shop. He was wearing a House Inspector pin on his jacket that Sylvia immediately noticed. She gave him a big smile, "Hello sir, how can I help you?"

"Just looking around," he answered. His eyes scanned the room, "What are the books for?" He asked grimly.

Sylvia took a breath, "My own personal collection, no room for them upstairs." She lied. She wasn't a book store and couldn't get caught classifying herself as it, or anything like it.

The man nodded, pulling some things off the shelf. "I'd like three onces of ginger root and two of the sage."

Sylvia nodded, getting her scale out, "What are you making?" She asked, trying for normal conversation.

"The ginger is for tea, the sage is for dinner." The man responded, the textbook answer.

Sylvia nodded again, writing down the prices for each ounce on a page. She multiplied them and then added them together in her head, "That will be twelve-fifty." She told the man, looking up.

He gave her a skeptical look, "What did you say your name was again?" He asked.

She hadn't, "Sylvia. Sylvia Blue."

He looked down at the paper, "Blue. That's linguistics, isn't it? You shouldn't be good at math."

Sylvia took a deep breath, resisting an eye roll. She knew if she didn't play this carefully, she could get caught for declassification. She didn't let her nerves show when she responded, "Arithmetic was my second best class. Would you like to see my chart?" She went to reach under the counter where she kept the yellow, laminated chart. He nodded, and she handed it over. Everyone got a chart when they graduated that explained their grades, best class to worst. If someone ever questioned your skill in a subject you had to show your chart. If you were better at math then your chart said, it gave evidence that you've changed, which wasn't allowed.

When he had looked it over enough, he handed it back, along with the money he owed.

"Thank you." He murmured, and left the shop.

Sylvia sat down, her nerves finally crashing over her, leaving her drained, that was a close one.

ooo

Liam shoved his hands deep into his pockets and ducked his head as he walked toward the wind. He only had four and a half blocks to walk, but it seemed like forever with the harsh wind of early fall. The weather had changed early this year, and he didn't like it.

Every community in The Witness Times were arranged in 1 mile by 1 mile squares. These squares were always in former cities, in parts that had been stabilized after the Awakening. Everything outside the city limits was still ruins, no one bothering to clean them up. Technically, these areas were forbidden, but that didn't mean scavengers and other curious kids didn't go wandering around there in the dark. No one ever knew what happened if you got caught, just the fact that you weren't ever seen again. You had broken the Code of Classification.

When you first become part of The House, you immediately start your life as a Witness. You graduate on Karma Day, and after that you go on to live in a community. According to the Reining Powers and The House, nothing happened to you before your time as a Witness. You only exist as part of The House; you go through schooling, graduate, and start a life in the community. Therefore, all you have ever known is the existence of your school, and then your community.

Liam thought all this over as he rounded the corner to get to work, especially with Karma Day coming up, he had been thinking a lot recently about The House and the system in general.

As he walked he took in the gray, hazy sky. He sidestepped the same brick pile he did every day. He kept his eyes low; he didn't want to see the broken skyscrapers that loomed in the distance. It was all eerie to him. The windows taped up to keep out the cold, the leaky pipes attached to apartments. His footsteps matched the *drip, drip, drip* of those pipes on 5th avenue.

He passed old signs hung outside of shops, paint peeling off of walls, a lack of graffiti. They lived in a very clean city because it was Clementine's city. It was just damp, gray, and tired. Rundown was a good word for it, but that word wasn't in the dictionary.

He knew that he shouldn't remember things before he became a Witness, but he did, he couldn't stop it. And he knew Sylvia did too, they had definitely talked about it all before. Sylvia knew how wrong the system felt to Liam, and he knew she felt the same way. Only difference between them was that she was always smart enough to skirt around the topic, and offered opinions only when directly asked. Liam however would just always come right out and say what he meant, a trait that often got him in trouble.

He moved his brick-like feet down the sidewalk, quiet thumps along an otherwise silent street.

The second O in Liams name was his occupation; objectives. Objectives were people who worked straight for The House, which for Liam was pretty amusing, seeing as he had so many questions that weren't allowed to be asked. Even more ironic was the fact that he was the writer of his Communities news report. A paper sent out twice a week to all the citizens, carrying the latest words from the Reining Powers. For him, writing was his passion. His best school subject was in fact, Occupational Writing (For frivolous fiction writing could never be categorically classified; and therefore a course was never offered for it).

Liam crossed the empty street and climbed the four, cold stone steps leading to his office building. He shoved the large black door open and it moved with a squawk, stubborn against the old wooden floors and hinges. He took in the scent of paper, ink, and wax. This was his second favorite smell, his first being the mixture of spices that always encompassed Sylvia.

Sylvia, he wondered how she was doing as he hung his coat up, all but one of the seven hooks already adorned with a series of heavy coats and scarves and hats. There was something haunting in the air today, something that had happened a few years before when they had graduated. Something familiar. But he was shaken out of his thoughts by a whip of straight black hair in his face.

"We were wondering when you planned on gracing us with your presence," Chaeronea's gray eyes glared at him annoyingly, seething through her black business suit. Liam's workers slowly moved along with their work, nervous of doing something to upset Chaeronea further.

Liam never backed down to Chaeronea, she couldn't touch him, as much as she wanted to. "It's nice to see you too, Chaeronea." He smiled at her, in his *you don't bother me* mannerism. "I trust you had a good weekend?"

She opened her mouth to speak but was intentionally interrupted by Liam, "That's great Chaeronea, but I really think we should be getting down to work, hm?" And with that Liam strode into his office, not bothering to hold the door open for the stunned women behind him. He sat down at his desk and took out his writing pad, followed by his glasses. He always felt so official sitting behind *his* desk. He didn't quite know what about the light colored wood object made him feel so powerful, it just did, the way a crown made a King feel powerful. Sylvia would laugh when he mentioned it.

"Like usual, we trust you have someone to take notes on this week's meeting, and those notes-"

"-will be published in the paper to go out tomorrow. Yes Chaeronea, we go over this every week." Liam rolled his eyes, always starting off Monday mornings with meetings with Chaeronea, getting the same old, rehearsed speech.

"I know, but if *you* mess up, it's on *both* of us." She looked annoyingly into his eyes. She was a strict ruler follower, not daring to cross any lines but instead daring to hate on those who did. Liam didn't much care for her.

"Besides that, as you know, tomorrow is Karma Day." She rolled her eyes at the dramatic name most people used to describe graduation. "The House wants an article about it on the second page, titled, 'New generation of community members graduate.'" Liam groaned, and Chaeronea gave him a small sympathetic smile, "Boring, I know. But they want what they want."

They continued going through the requirements and outline for Tuesday's paper. Liam took notes, writing down the words that had to be included and the ones that could absolutely, under no circumstances be included. He typed up headlines and formatting, and after an hour and a half, he emerged from his office and posted the instructions on a billboard. All his employees looked up from whatever they were doing to hear Liam announce everyone's articles.

"Charles you're on the new Bakery opening up on second. Matthew, I want you to do the write up on when the construction will be finished near the office district. Jenn, why don't you take the Reining Powers newest ancouments on schooling?"

"I was actually going to do that story on the community-"

"Yeah, sorry, that story has been cut, too much room for conflict. I'll take the Karma Day story and Lily, you'll be taking notes at the meeting like usual. We're going for light, air tight and structured. Avoid any mention of fruits this week, and looks like that's all, let me know if you have questions." Liam worked in a kind but firm manner. It was only by chance that he had gotten the job, and it took him awhile to earn everyone's trust and respect. Some days he had gone home to Sylvia defeated because a deadline hadn't been met, or he had to write a story himself instead of the person who he had assigned it to. He remembered how Sylvia always made him feel better, wrapping him in her arms, and with her help he calmed down and worked out a plan.

Chaeroena had left a few minutes before, heading back to her own office across town. Liam headed back to his desk and sat down to work. The whole day went relatively well, and before he knew it he was packing up and putting on his coat. Everyone else had already ducked their heads into his office, saying their goodbyes, nights, and see you tomorrows. He turned off the lights, and the glass gridded window panes shone blue with the outside light of night. When he opened the door, his shadow danced into the office, a reminder of the time he spent in that building. He dragged the door shut behind him with a scrape, killing his shadow along the way.

ooo

Liam walked into the spice shop, the bells introducing his entrance. He looked around and was greeted with the familiar warmth of Sylvia and her presence.

"Hey! Let me just grab my stuff and we can walk down to the meeting." Sylvia said, pushing her hair behind both ears and grabbing her keys from next to the register. Liam just smiled at her, sometimes he just liked taking the time to watch her. The way she moved around the small area, the way she owned her steps and knew where everything was. She grabbed her purple coat and put her arms into it as she walked out the door Liam was holding for her. She locked the shop with her key and smiled up at him, really taking in his expression for the first time since he got back. He looked tired but happy, she could relate.

They walked hand in hand to the Town Meeting Hall, about 7 blocks from where they lived. It was cold, but bundled up together they braced themselves against the cold air. They talked about everyone and everything that had happened that day. Sylvia didn't bring up the man who entered her shop earlier that day; no need to worry Liam before a meeting, it was better to just wait. So she enjoyed his company, realizing she had missed him more than she thought, and him thinking the same.

CHAPTER TWO

Sylvia climbed the dusty, chilling steps of the attic one by one after her sister. Her bare feet were cold, but the air surrounding her was warm as she moved up the steps. Her right hand was clutching the steeply inclining rail, and her left hand was engulfed in her sister's hand who walked in front of her.

Her sister was tall for her age, with shoulder length curly dark brown hair; hazel eyes shone over her shoulder as she looked back towards her. Sylvia watched as her sister's purple dress swung up and down with each stair, and she looked down to see if her own pink dress was doing the same.

When they reached the top of the stairs, she sat down on the hardwood floor. Dust seemed to coat everything, but she didn't mind. She was enchanted at the new place before her, a place that had always existed right above her head. She stood up to run her hands along a rack of coats, carefully covered in plastic for reasons she didn't know. She walked through a maze of boxes, different shapes and sizes, with neat letters printed along the side, she liked the shapes and the way they formed.

When she rounded another set of boxes, Sylvia found her sister standing in front of a small, striped box. She watched as her sister, Wallace, pulled out a long white, sheer piece of fabric. On the top of which sat little white pearls and lace flowers. Wallace held the odd fabric piece as if it might break any second, and precariously placed it on her head. The fabric fell in front of her sister's beautiful face, her hazel eyes still visible through the shear wall, the flowers placed gently in the back of her hair.

Sylvia had seen hats like that before, they were called veils, and brides wore them on their wedding day. But she wondered what other purpose they served. The hat Wallace wore on her head wasn't like the knitted hats her Mother gave her to keep against the cold, the flaps pulled down over her ears and the inside fleece warming her cheeks.

Wallace turned towards the dusty old mirror with the wooden frame, perched in the corner of the attic. She moved the shear fabric up and over her head, and saw her little sister Sylvia watching through the mirror.

"This was our great grandmother's veil." Wallace started, "Momma wore it when she married Dad, and Momma's mother wore it when she married grandpa, and our great-grandma when she married our great-grandpa. Someday, I'm going to wear this veil when I marry the man of my dreams." Her sister spoke to her reflection in the mirror, as if to explain it to herself.

Afterwards, Wallace replaced the veil into the box. She carefully tied the box back over the striped cover, and using both hands, placed it on the top shelf of the bookcase.

"It will be safe here," she nodded her head.

Although she was small, Sylvia would never forget the look on her sister's face when she was wearing the veil. It was a look of contentment, of hope, a bright future.

ooo

Sylvia sat there for hours, she knew she did because the clock continued to tick at her feet. When she moved, her bones cracked and her neck was stiff. Her face was sticky, dried salty tears covering her cheeks like makeup. She walked down the aisle with a blank mind. She wasn't thinking anything, she just knew she couldn't be there at that moment, and if she didn't move now, she never would.

Sylvia walked down the aisle, back towards the door. She was wearing black converse with white laces, a decision about the wedding her sister had made that she actually liked. She personally loved the red dress - black sneaker look.

As she walked, her shoes stepped on insulation, roof tiles, glass shards; nothing registered in her brain. When she got to the door, her shaking right hand reached out to take the handle, and the door opened smoothly. The light didn't scare or shock her, she had become used to it while lying on the carpet, but something else made the hairs on her arms stand up.

She stood on the top step of the church, bright white marble below her. Her dress was powdered with dust and ripped at the hem. Her eyes were bright, red, and puffy. Her hair fell over her shoulders, mangled, some parts stiff with old hairspray and other parts frizzy, happy to free themselves from the rest. Her shoes were unlaced, the deep black color of the fabric stained like her dress. She was a wreck, she mirrored the world around her.

When Sylvia walked down the steps, down the street to the town, she didn't notice the broken world around her. The ruins of the gas station, the library, the memorial statue in the park. Rafters and glass and bricks laid in the street she walked on. If she had been able to think clearly, she would have seen the lack of people, the lack of noise. That's what was so different about the outside, everything was silent. Even the explosions in the background had seized.

When Sylvia turned the corner, she heard something. A new noise in this silent blackhole. She found herself staring into the window of a shop; a television shop. Her town was unique, as they still had these little shops instead of giant chain stores. In the window display, TV's of all shapes and sizes flashed with the same image, the same stream. Sylvia focused on one in the middle, oblivious to how untouched this one building was. The screen showed a man, darker skin, bald, and wearing glasses. He stood on a podium, and below him a white stripe displayed his name; Chairman Clementine.

Sylvia recognized him immediately. He had been in the news for the past nine months, negotiating with the President over trade matters. He had always threatened war.

When Sylvia realized what had happened, she almost fell over. Her hand went out to find the glass window in front of her, and she stabilized herself against it to hear the man speaking.

"Residents, do not be afraid. There is no reason to be afraid, for we have started a new era. All of you are a part of a new group of people which is to be called, The House. We will not have countries in this new world, we

will not have districts, we will have The House, and all of the residents of this world will be part of The House. Do you hear that everyone? You are a part of something. I congratulate each and every one of you." Sylvia's head was swimming, her ideas spun.

"We will all live under a peaceful law, that law is classification." Sylvia found herself getting dizzy, *"Residents, hear me when I say this is how we prevent everything that has previously gone wrong in this world. Classification is the only way. It is an essential element which we will practice everyday. With this new rule, our new rule, we can stop horrible acts of loss, sadness, anger, treason, kidnapping, murder, every horrifying act that you have experienced before."* Claps rose from the background, cheers, calls of admiration.

"With that said, there are some people who have decided to fight against our new world." Clementine's voice shifted to a more serious, dire tone, *"We do not know how long their struggle against us will last, only that that time period will be known as the Awakening. We need to group together and fight against the ones who threaten to disrupt our classification. We can not let them ruin our new world."*

"Together, we will create a world worth living in. There is no reason to disrupt this process, because this process is the right way. And why disrupt what is right?" Chairman Clementine moved his eyes to meet the

camera. Applause rose from the audience, and then he began to move offstage. The feed wiggled, and started over again.

Sylvia sank down to the ground, her legs were shaking so much they couldn't hold her. She couldn't control what was happening to her, how she felt, anything.

When asked to describe how she felt that day, she would only use one word: suffocated.

CHAPTER THREE

When Liam and Sylvia got to the meeting house it was already bustling with energy. Liam quickly retreated into his shell, feeling overwhelmed. But Sylvia was right there next to him, and she threaded her arm through his. Together they went around saying their hellos and how are yous. Sylvia knew everyone, and everyone knew Sylvia. Liam on the other hand sometimes found himself face to face with a person he just *knew* he had never seen before, but they always claimed they knew him. His strategy was to smile and nod and let Sylvia take the lead, which she always gladly did.

Liam and Sylvia found their way to their seats, fifth aisle from the back and in the middle. He looked for Lily, who was stationed to the right of the stage, with paper and pencil in hand. He relaxed into his chair with Sylvia next to him.

"Turns out, the Macs, you know the older couple across the street? They're taking in one of the kids tomorrow at Karma Day. Isn't that nice?"

"Yeah, it really is. I wonder if Matilda knows her. Speaking of which, is her space upstairs all ready? I know I was supposed to help you with that... there's just this story I got really into at work, but I can help when we get home."

"Lee, it's all good. I got it done when business was slow, thank you though," and she gave him an adorable smile and a hand squeeze. She stood up and shook a neighbours hand across the row of chairs, they exchanged some pleasantries but fell silent when Chaeronea started climbing the stairs of the stage. Sylvia sat down next to Liam, back straight and eyes examining Chaeronea movements. Sylvia didn't care much for Chaeronea, their personalities clashed. While Sylvia lived freely in the world, happily making friends and knowing everyone, Chaeronea took a different approach, staring down at everyone below her. She was committed to The House and following rules.

Even though Sylvia disliked Chaeronea, she took the time to try and understand her, a quality Liam admired. He just chose the sarcastic snappy lines when it came to talking to Chaeronea. Liam watched Sylvia's face as she watched Chaeronea, and Sylvia turned to him without taking her eyes off the stage.

"Lei è nervosa, sta succedendo qualcosa di grosso." *She's nervous, something big is happening,*

Sylvia said in italian, her favorite language to speak in.

Liam inwardly smiled at Sylvia's observation and language abilities, and dragged his eyes to the podium as the room quieted.

Chaeronea started, "Welcome, Community members, to Tuesday night meetings. As you all know, we have these meetings every Tuesday and Friday nights, that is: two out of six days of the week. The Reigning Powers appreciate your attendance, as members of this community and members of the even bigger House, your attendance helps build an environment of fellowship."

Liam resisted an eye roll as he recited word by word the first part of her speech, the same introduction she used every day. Every community had a meeting like this on Tuesday and Friday nights, and as Chaeronea said, all community members were part of The House. The House existed in place of what Khaos members would call a government.

"Now, to talk about today's announcements, tomorrow is graduation for the class of 2021 from the community school. Everyone has the day off to attend the ceremony. Furthermore, as is tradition, all the graduates will be going to stay with a community family for the designated three months.

We trust that you welcome these new community members with open arms, and help them learn the lay of the land and the ways of this community."

A rise of applause rose from the audience, Liam and Sylvia clapped along with everyone, soft thuds getting drowned by a roar.

"In other news, the Agricultural group is working on raising our supplies of fruits. You may see a decline in the next week or so, but it is only because the Agricultural Groups need the fruit for testing and growing more." There was more clapping from the chairs, Liam mimed along. He zoned out for most of the rest of the speech, examining the meeting room instead. The walls were coated in a cerulean paint, with the long windows breaking the walls in vertical lines. A soft haze of light landed on the floor, almost enough to cast a shadow. The floor was a light hardwood, contrary to the red-brown chairs in lines along that same floor, with an isle along the middle. Liam constantly wondered if this place reminded Sylvia of the church she was in the first day of the Awakening. Although she didn't speak of it often, Liam knew how that part of her life haunted her. His own experiences haunted his dreams too. Sylvia was better at dealing with those parts of her, Liam just locked them away in a box never to be touched. Matilda had a different approach, she talked about them like they were stories, myths whispered around the fire. It almost made him uncomfortable, not knowing exactly how to comfort her if she needed it, but at the same time he honored her bravery in that way.

"Lastly, the Reining Powers have decided to add a new enforcement for everyone's safety in this community. Starting Wednesday, as is the day after graduation, patrolmen will be on our perimeter."

Liam's thoughts were broken by the change in Chaeronea's voice as she talked. Whispers broke out on the floor of the meeting hall, completely unusual in such a professional setting. Chaeroena glanced down at the podium, and shuffling her pages around, started again.

"We want to stress that this is only for your safety as community members. It is a new protocol that will be tested for an undetermined amount of time. I can not disclose the full reasoning for this new addition, but, to make the transition smoother, the Reining Powers have agreed to let you meet with the patrolman for each of your blocks. They will come to your houses on Wednesday to introduce themselves to each and every one of you. Please make sure you are all home at 6 o'clock on Wednesday night, after work, to meet with them. They are very happy to meet each and every one of you."

Chaeroena gave the crowd a proud smile, leaving everyone feeling partly confused, and partly content in the new, surprising edition.

"Thank you very much. The Reining Powers wish you all a satisfactory week. We'll meet again on Friday night." Chaeronea picked up her papers and left the stage, black heels clicking along the wood, quickly drowned out with the scraping of chairs on the floor and the rise of voices. Liam and Sylvia said their goodbyes and hand in hand walked out in silence. They stayed in an appropriate silence for the first few blocks to their house, until Sylvia spoke.

"As much as I dislike Chaeronea," Sylvia started hesitantly, "She handles pressure pretty well. Her speech was very well written. Although, that's pretty obvious considering-"

"Considering the Reining Powers A. wouldn't have chosen her if she wasn't a good writer and B. if she couldn't adjust her words to match what they want to say." Liam finished for her.

"First off, nice job jumping in with the end of that sentence, that's usually my thing." Sylvia side glanced up at him, and he gave her a smirk. "And true. No wonder they picked her to be their government-"

"Errrr. Try again. Word. Is. Not. Recognizable." Liam started in a robotic voice, "Error. Error. Error."

"Alright! I get it." Sylvia said through laughter, putting her hands up in surrender. Liam poked her with his elbow smiling, and they went back to holding hands. "As I was saying, it's no wonder they picked Chaeronea to head up their communications department. She's the strictest person ever; She would never do anything against The House."

"Or, has her job just made her the strict person that she is, in fear of her life?" Liam raised an eyebrow, playing devil's advocate as always, and Sylvia loved it.

"True. I guess it depends on if you stand on the side of The House, or the revolution." She threw her hand in the air in a fist, although she whispered the last part of the sentence, out of fear of others hearing it. They both knew there was no revolution, but it was fun to think about, to talk and joke about it.

"After the revolution, everyone will eat warm chocolate chip cookies every day."

"After the revolution, we will raise 3 kids."

"After the revolution, you'll become a doctor and I'll start my own newspaper."

"After the revolution, we will go on vacations, swim in the ocean and sit on the hot sand. We'll ride a ferris wheel and ski down a mountain."

It was a game they played with each other from time to time, whenever their reality was too much for them to take.

Sylvia and Liam reached their house and unlocked the door to the familiar smell of spices. They took off their coats and hung them on the pins behind the staircase. Sylvia locked the shop while Liam went to start the fire upstairs. She grabbed a jar of peppermint tea bags, her favorite wide blue mug, and Liam's tall green one.

The rest of the night passed with good food, laughter, and card games. Sylvia made up the cot in the corner with new sheets for Matilda, who would be coming tomorrow, and Liam and Sylvia fell asleep in front of the fire like they usually did. Later in the night, Liam lifted Sylvia into his arms and moved her to the bed that sat inlaid in a bay window. She looked so peaceful in sleep, and Liam wished he had a camera to capture the moment. the Awakening had taken his camera, his computer, everything. the Awakening had given him Sylvia, but taken everything else from him.

Was he upset and angry, or content and happy with the way things had worked out? He fell asleep, arms wrapped around his one true love, the only love he had ever experienced.

ooo

"Domination is how we control the classification and keep peace over the land. Dominance is something to be proud of-"

"No. It's domination is how we control the classification and keep peace over the land. Dominance is something to *stay* proud of and it is a community members job to stay firm in our one and only belief that this is the way to keep the world safe. Liam we've been over this!" Sylvia forcibly whispered at him. They sat in the common room for their grade, young Sylvia's hair up in a messy bun, Liam wearing an oversized gray sweatshirt. The room was dark, due to the late hour of night. No one was supposed to be up, but Sylvia was determined to have Liam pass the test this time.

"I know, I know. But these rules are so complicated! Why do they have to be so long?" Liam sat up from his previous position, where his head had been dangling off the couch with his feet on the top of the pillows. He moved his legs to rest on Sylvia's lap, who was sitting criss cross next to him, paper in hand. It would have been an eerie atmosphere if the soft hum of the heater didn't play in the background. Everything else was quiet, no footsteps or whispers other than their own. It was so quiet you would be able to hear the shadows creep along the floor.

"I know Lee. But if you don't pass this time they'll send you away," She paused for a moment, "to ... to who knows where," Sylvia's voice cracked near the end, and a few tears rolled down her cheeks. Her cheeks burned with a blush of embarrassment that grew up her neck. She pulled her lavender long sleeves down into the palms of her hands, wrapping her knuckles with the fabric.

"Hey, hey." Liam started, suddenly awake even though it was late at night. "V, I'm not going anywhere, I'm gonna ace that test." He moved next to her and wiped at her tears, holding her face with his hands. "It would be impossible to fail, considering I have the world's best teacher." He smiled. .

Sylvia cracked a smile at the compliment, "I know, I'm sorry. It's just that I haven't really been sleeping well and I'm so stressed I kind of get..." She didn't need to finish the sentence, Liam knew she got emotional when she didn't sleep well.

"It's okay, really. One more time, I swear I'm going to get it."

"Alright. What's the first rule?"

They stayed there for most of the night going over the exact words to The House's constitution, whispered laughs and urgencies. The next day, Liam took his test and passed, only missing one word in one phrase, which was allowed under the rules of the test. Sylvia took Liam by the hand and led him up the secret staircase to the roof, the one no one knew existed because it was hidden behind the kitchen, where only the cooks worked. Sylvia had discovered it one day when she volunteered to be a kitchen helper.

They laid on the rooftop under stars and a full moon on a ratty green quilt Liam had snatched from the pile of confiscated things. Both of them realized it was risky, but neither seemed to care. This was their one, tiny act of rebellion.

Sylvia had been at the school for 2 years, while Liam started only seven months ago, but Sylvia just couldn't imagine, and didn't want to remember what it was like before Liam, without Liam.

Legs spread out before them on the blanket, arms supporting them from behind. Sylvia's head rested on Liam's shoulder, and his arm curled along her back.

"I'm glad you passed." Sylvia started.

"It's all because of you." Liam answered sincerely.

"Thank you."

"But *seriously*, you have such a hard time remembering things!" Sylvia laughed with him.

"I know, I know. It's more like, some things I don't want to remember, you know?" Liam told her.

"Yeah. I know what you mean." She moved her head back to his shoulder.

They sat in silence, enjoying each other's company, the warmth of each other's arms.

"It was a Saturday, and I was wearing my pajamas and watching TV on the living room couch. I remember it was Tom and Jerry. I wanted to change the channel, but my little brother, Henry, wanted to keep the cartoon on. We were arguing, just like all siblings do, when we heard this huge noise, like a giant boom coming from down the road."

"Liam, you don't have to tell me this." She stopped him, raising her head to meet his eyes.

"No. You told me your story, I want to share mine with you. It's an important part of me, just like you are." He never broke her gaze, and Sylvia slowly nodded her head, not pressuring him to speak on. Her head found his shoulder again.

"My mom went out on the porch, and as soon as she came back in I knew something was wrong, like, *really wrong*. Her eyes seemed to be on fire, and she started yelling at all of us. That's what really scared me. Not the boom, or the way everyone started screaming on our road, but the fact that my mom raised her voice. Never in my life had she done that before."

Liam took a deep breath before continuing, "My mom rushed us all down to the basement. I was trying to calm down my little brother, even though I was freaking out just as much as he was. He didn't understand why we were downstairs instead of watching cartoons.

"My family was one of the only blocks on our street with a basement and my mom knew it. So she left to go get the neighbors. My brother was crying, and I kept telling him that she would come back. Over and over I told him it would be fine. And then he started asking about his dad, my step-dad. He had gone to work that morning because the office needed him, and Henry just kept asking where he was, if he was coming, if he would stay in the basement with us."

"Did he?" Sylvia whispered.

Liam shook his head, "We don't know what happened to him. He had no idea that when he left for work that day, there would be no home to return to."

Sylvia moved closer to him. He continued, "My mom came back a few minutes later with the older couple across the street, Mr. and Mrs. Phern, and the single businessman from down the block,

Greg Jordan. My mom locked us in there and started grabbing blankets and food from cabinets. She had been storing stuff ever since I was born, when my real dad took off. I never knew why, but at that moment I was very happy about it."

Sylvia took Liam's hand in her own, waiting, and he kept going. "Henry and I gave the couch to Mr.Jordan, and set up some sleeping bags in the corner. My mom rushed to blow up the air mattress for Mr and Mrs. Phern before the power went out. I wrapped Henry in a blanket because he was shivering uncontrollably. The Pherns sat on the bed comforting each other, and I remember Mr.Jordan pacing the floor, back and forth, back and forth. I thought he was going to set the carpet on fire with the friction." Liam allowed himself a small laugh, but it was soaked in a sadness Sylvia knew well.

"Explosions went off all around us, and every time we heard that awful noise we jumped. It was not a sound you get used to, as you know. Mr. Jordan, it was like he was eating himself alive, his face so contorted. Eventually he picked up the radio and turned it on." He took another deep breath, memories flooding through his mind, breaking the damn he had put up these last few months. "The radio had only one station working, and over and over it played the same thing; *Classification is the universal way to keep peace. Classification is the universal way to keep peace.* Over and over again, but Mr. Jordan wouldn't turn it off, no matter how many times my mom asked.

"Eventually, they started playing more things on the radio, and we learned what happened and what was going on. We stayed in that basement for as long as we could, for as long as our food would last us. Mr. Jordan, he couldn't take it for very long. He made it four months before he went crazy and left. He kept shouting in his sleep and pacing the room all day. It was scary for Henry and I, but my mom always helped calm everyone down. She was a saint. After about eight months, we started to go out a little at a time. We didn't know what was safe, we didn't know if there were others like us, and we didn't know how to buy the things we were running out of. The Pherns never left, neither did Henry, he was just too young. I went out with my mom when we needed things, and sometimes I went out all by myself when my mom couldn't leave everyone. We spent the whole two year Awakening down there. Mrs. Phern passed away, and after that Mr. Phern was very quiet. Henry went whole weeks without speaking, either he didn't have the energy, or he was just too depressed. I did everything I could to cheer him up, making paper toys, or drums with old cans, anything, he just wasn't the same.

"When The House found us, it was right after the Awakening finished and people were going around collecting survivors. They stormed the basement, and I haven't seen my mom or Henry since then." Liam struggled to take a deep, shaky breath. Silver tears silently ran down his cheeks, "The rest you know. I came to school because I was strong enough to. I don't know what happened to my mom, or to Henry. But I think of them almost every day, I don't want to forget what they looked like, who they were. I don't want to forget them, but I want to forget everything else."

Sylvia and Liam had now moved to sit cross legged in front of each other. Sylvia wiped Liam's tears, but she was crying herself. They took each other's hands and leaned their foreheads together; the eye of their world's storm.

CHAPTER FOUR

At 6 AM Matilda woke up to the sound of horns, like everyday. She stretched her arms above her head, pointed her toes, and shook out the cramps in her body before getting up and putting on her black glasses. She pulled the light green blanket up to the top of her bed and fluffed her pillow; the last time she would ever have to do that. She showered and changed, barely making eye contact with the other students around her. She wore a rust red tunic with matching leggings and tied her shoulder length blonde hair in a high ponytail using a strip of fabric. After checking the time, she grabbed her backpack and finished packing.

She grabbed her secret knick-knacks and odds and ends from under the bed and carefully wrapped them in her clothing, placing them in the green backpack. A blue green crystal she found in an old antique shop, a brass ring from her mom, a pair of fingerless gloves Sylvia had given her before she graduated, a photo Liam had given her of a pair of llamas. She remembered when he had found it and how funny he thought the picture was.

With her prized possessions stored away, she shouldered her backpack and walked down the hall, passed the other rooms, through the common room, and out the door. Her eyes scanned everything top to bottom, taking everything in for the last time.

When she stepped through the door, the light from the arena hurt, and it took a minute for her eyes to adjust. Squinting, she found her way to the circle of chairs on the floor of the stadium. Large rows of bench seating rose from the floor, five stories high, but those seats weren't for her, or any of the graduates. They were for the community members, and she calmed herself by remembering that Sylvia and Liam would sit somewhere up there.

Matilda found her seat next to Joseph Karl. The seats went alphabetically, with last names grouped together. Matilda was happy she was the only Kurt. If there were more, her teachers would try to convince her that they were family, even though they only shared a last name that was given to them. She knew her mother's last name, it had been Kuot. Matilda was proud she was able to obtain three of the same letters as her mother.

When Matilda sat down, she slid her bag under her seat like they had been instructed to do. She put both feet on the floor, shoulder length apart, with her back straight and her hands folded in her lap.

"When *we* graduated, I had to basically hold V's feet to the floor." Liam had told her when he and Sylvia had come to visit her last week. "She wanted so badly to sit criss-cross, cross her legs, *anything*." Sylvia had started laughing, punching him lightly on the shoulder, defending herself, only fake offended.

Matilda thought they were so perfect together, and was happy she was spending her three months with them. The memory made her smile, and then she remembered where she was and re-pasted her mask on. The room was eerie and silent, the benches looming above everyone, waiting for a show, waiting for people. Matilda was also waiting for people, waiting for it all to be over, waiting to start a new normal. Five. This would be her fifth time beginning a new normal. The first one when her mom joined The House before The House even existed. The second when the Awakening started. The third when she began school and met Liam and Sylvia, losing her mom in the process. The fourth when Liam and Sylvia left, and now the fifth. She wondered if The House never existed, if the Awakening never happened, how many normals she would have had by now.

OOO

"Mi ricordo quando ci siamo laureati," *I remember when we graduated.* Liam whispered into Sylvia's ear. She blushed, memories flooding her. It had been a day of mixed emotions.

As they walked, she fidgeted with the hem of her shirt. Liam knew all her habits by heart; her mindless twirling of hair, how she pulled at the skin around her thumbs, how she tapped her fingers when she was tired.

Liam had her memorized, and he liked it that way.

Tucking her hair behind her ear, she smiled up at him. She wanted to tell him something. She wanted to tell him how nervous she was. She wanted to fidget but she actively tried not to. Every step they walked closer and closer to the place she spent six years in.

She took a deep breath, exhaling her nerves about Karma Day. The thought that something so horrible could be happening without anyone fighting against it made her sick to her stomach.

When Liam first met Sylvia, he had noticed an air of confidence around her instead of the shadow of sadness that followed most people these days. She still had that confidence now, even with her nerves, it was always there. Liam had learned when the atmosphere was getting a little thin because he wanted to be there for her when it did.

"Tell me something V." Liam said, interested in words filling the space around them.

Sylvia thought a minute, distracted from her other thoughts, exactly what Liam had wanted, "The first Shakespeare book I ever read said, 'Hell is empty and all the devils are here.'" She started to laugh, "I honestly think that's why I fell in love with Shakespeare" Sylvia's wide eyes met Liams, as he burst out laughing at the randomness of Sylvia's response.

"Really?" He questioned.

"Totally. In *The Tempest*. All these important people were on a boat, and suddenly a huge storm came over them. And then, the boat started to catch on fire, while it was still raining. Everyone got super freaked out, and honestly I don't blame them. It's pretty hilarious though."

Liam found himself looking up into the sky, seeing the top floors of buildings as he walked, something he usually didn't do. He started swinging their intertwined hands, "You're something else Sylvia Blue." He smiled. Her ability to make him forget everything around them, everything that was happening, that had happened, was amazing.

She was his calm place.

As they were walking, Liam thought about what Shakespeare had written. Water and fire, two elements always against each other. Two elements; each, their weakness, the other. His thoughts were punctuated by Sylvia talking about the new teas she made, and the new people who came into her shop. He was listening to her. He was interested in her. But he was thinking.

The people on the boat had just been in the middle of a battle for dominance. Wasn't that true for everyone?

○○○

Graduation was always very short.

And terrifying - it was called Karma Day for a reason.

Giant lights hang in the air glaring at you, making you sweat. Tons of people lined up to see you, to watch the show. Those same people who can make layers upon layers of noise, and then fall silent with one single hand. All of your senses are heightened on Karma Day, all of your fears are enlarged.

It's the day you could die.

The day your classification couldn't be necessary anymore.

Liam and Sylvia found their seats, which were pretty close to the top of the stadium. Each year you were part of the community you moved down a row in the stadium, closer and closer to the main event. The seats were hard concrete benches and always hurt Liam's back. Right on que, Sylvia brought her arm around Liam's back and settled her hand on the concrete of the seat; a brace for Liam. Neither of them mentioned it, they both knew he appreciated her. Around them you could feel the heaviness of chaos.

Not a destructive chaos, but a feeling of raw emotion, something dangerous and real. Sylvia felt it in her toes, so she leaned up against Liam's side.

"Cosa farei se venisse scelta?" *What would we do if she got picked?* She asked, thinking of all the possibilities.

"Non succederà il, mio amore" *That won't happen, my love.* Liam replied, being the deal-with-a-problem-when-it-comes guy. Sylvia didn't mind his response, it made her feel secure. Her eyes scanned the circle of graduates, before finding their way back to Matilda's face. They had chosen a spot where they could see her features, and she looked the same as always. Her glasses were pushed up the bridge of her nose and she sat very still, perfect posture. Liam's eyes went between watching Matilda and looking over at Sylvia.

"I think that..." Liam started, but he was cut off by all the lights going off. A swift light cut off at the seams. A rush of whispers filled the stadium. No matter how many times it happened, how many times he told himself it was fine, Liam could never get used to it. The enormity of the dark around him was eerie, too much to be comfortable with. He reached over Sylvia's lap and grabbed her hand. A rush of cool air rose from the floor, and stillness settled around them, landing in his ears, his eyes, on his fingernails.

After the initial reaction, the stadium fell silent. A quiet so immense that it felt heavy on people's shoulders, and they begged their eyes to adjust to the dark so that they could have some control over the pressure coming down on them; No one dared to even shuffle their feet. Intimidation was not a strong enough word to describe the immense darkness that stretched before them, and as Liam sat there he tried words out on his tongue to see if they fit.

Threatening.

Unnerving.

Terrorizing.

That was it, and just like that he was brought back to when he and Sylvia were graduating.

"Those terrorists probably just pick it out of a hat!"

"V, v." Liam tried to calm her, *"It's fine.You're fine, I'm fine, we're fine! This is going to be over soon, and no one is going to be hurt, okay?"*

She raised her eyebrows, *"Tomorrow is literally Karma Day Lee, the day when the decisions you made in school are weighed against you. What if I should have been better at Agriculture? What if they pick Linguistics? What if they pick-"* But Liam couldn't hear any more of it, he grabbed her waist and pulled her into a kiss, taking her by surprise, one she quickly leaned into.

No more words were passed between them, but nothing had to be. Both were worried about Karma Day, but on the actual day, Sylvia didn't show any nerves at all; Other than the fact Liam had to beg her to keep both of her feet on the ground, as was protocol. When their ceremony had started, Liam kept his eyes on Sylvia who was sitting across the circle from him.

He was snapped from his thoughts as the lights turned back on, brighter than ever. In a normal situation, everyone would groan at the bright light, but this wasn't a normal situation. Fear escalated around the room. Eyes darting to find the student they were supposed to be bringing home.

Seeing if their student was still there.

Liam's eyes had never left the spot Matilda was sitting. He let out a breath he was holding, she was still there.

She was still there.

He felt Sylvia relax beside him, exhaling. He looked over at her, her eyes relieved. Muffled shrieks and wet eyes were around them as people took in the empty chairs, the missing people. Liam could feel a sadness in Sylvia and he knew why. He knew why he still felt an ache in his body. Even though Matilda was fine, there were others that weren't.

Liam quickly moved to watch Matilda's face. Her eyes glazed over half the circle, searching for someone, seeing who was still there and who wasn't. Her stare settled on a boy, her eyes changing from concern to relief. Her whole face relaxed. Whoever the boy was, he hadn't been taken, and Matilda was happy about that.

Liam's body tensed, becoming protective, something inside him he felt whenever Matilda was around. Even though she was twenty now, he still saw the ten year-old he had met over ten years before. The Matilda he had first met was broken.

No one would hurt her again, he would make sure of it.

Sylvia sighed and rested her head on Liam's shoulder. She would be quiet the rest of the day in the wake of the tragedy.

When the commotion died down and people tried to silence their tears so as to not draw attention, a video of Chairman Clementine was projected onto the only flat wall. Some teachers and important people who Sylvia recognized stood to the sides of the video. She saw Chaeronea standing to the right, closest to the screen.

"Graduates!" The video of Clementine started, *"There should be no tears today, for it is a day of celebration. And how many of those do you get? Am I right?"* He chuckled, *"It is not everyday we have new people coming into our community!*

"Every one of you have important roles in this community, as you already know, and have known since the beginning of your life.

Life as a witness, he meant, Liam thought to himself.

"These roles are no big deal," Sylvia rolled her eyes, Chairman Clementine was always very sarcastic, and she hated it, *"Just kidding! The roles you have been classified in are essential to your community, and your well being."* Seriousness rolled over his voice.

"Know, fellow community members, that the world outside your school walls is not as scary as it

might seem. When we keep order and peace, as we do now, we find that everything is perfect in classification. With that said, although some mistakes are allowed and required in school, they are not in a real community.

"But enough of that! Let's not spoil the day with unpleasantries! I will leave you with a quote, some words of wisdom from a very wise man, me; There is only one true happiness in life, classifying everything, until everything and everyone has its exact place."

After that, the screen went blank and Chaeronea stepped up to a podium. Sylvia sighed, waiting to fill her ears with more useless words.

"Hello Community members, thank you for being here today. Chairman Clementine said it wisely and perfectly, so I won't take up much of your time with this goodbye. Graduates, your teachers want to wish you a great life in the community. You have all worked hard to get to this point. I want to remind you of the three months you will spend with a community family, and that your jobs start in two days. We look forward to seeing how you help the community around you.

"One.

"Two.

"Three."

A singular clap rang through the air, coming from hundreds of hands.

Perfectly making one, unison sound.

ooo

Liam grabbed Matilda's bag from her, despite her protest about his bad back and how she could do it herself. They had left the school as quickly as possible and were walking back home, Matilda on Liam's left with Sylvia on his right. Liam held Sylvia's hand as they walked.

People streamed out of the school, turning in their respective directions to get home, graduates following. Matilda walked in awe of the world around her, so preciously new to her. She took in the way her feet sounded along the pavement, how the fall air smelled and how the buildings loomed above her.

"So, your space is all made up at our place, thanks to Sylvia." Liam started, he didn't like silence, even regular empty silence made him uncomfortable. He directed the comment to Matilda, even though he kept his gaze on the girl to his right. Her eyes met the toes of her shoes as she trailed along beside him.

Matilda waited a minute before she responded, both of them were trying to pry words from Sylvia, although she was oblivious to it. "Thanks! I really appreciate you taking me in, it would just be weird if I was with a family I didn't know."

"Mat, there is *no way* we would let you go anywhere but our home." Liam said, and put his arm around the girl.

She smiled and removed herself from his arms, comfortably walking free. She felt ready to live on her own.

"So just down that road is where you're going to be working."

"Oh, okay cool. How far is that from The House?"

"Not far at all, our building is just down this street and over to the left. Oh, and that's my office."

"So that's where all the fancy reporting happens," Matilda shot Liam a look.

"Ha. Yeah right. It's more like message relay."

"Well, it's still cool that you..."

"Who was it this time?" Sylvia interjected. She was still looking down, but she had asked the question Liam was afraid of asking, she always did, because she had to know. The question was the reason their conversation had an undertone of fear, of sadness. It was the reason the day was called Karma Day. It was the reason people tried to block the day from their memories. Matilda took a few moments, silent, looking to the ground.

"The Undertakers. It was a job this time."

Sylvia held onto Liam's hand a little tighter. They were her people. She thought, if she wasn't here, if her and a few more like her weren't here, then they still would be. The House would have had a spot for them.

Liam knew what she was thinking, "Non è colpa vostra." *It's not your fault.* He whispered to her, and when her green eyes met his, he felt a pain and a longing to help her.

"Non specificamente." *Not specifically.* She whispered.

Liam readjusted his hand with hers. The three of them walked the rest of the way home in silence, thinking the same thoughts.

Although no one knew where the category of the graduates went during Karma Day, and no one had hope they would ever come back. Rumors circulated, as they do. The main explanation of the disappearances was that some communities don't need certain people each year.

The year Liam and Sylvia graduated it had been the Agriculture jobs.

Last year it was the Arithmetic scholars.

This year, the Undertakers.

If Sylvia has just been two years younger, she would be gone today. That thought haunted Liam the rest of the night.

OOO

"You're kidding, right?!"

"No! It actually happened!" Sylvia replied to Matilda.

"Ha. Ha. Ha. Just laugh at my expense, why don't you?" Liam added.

"Awe Lee, we aren't laughing at you, just with you." Sylvia gave Liam a look to melt his heart. They were curled up in front of the fire, with Matilda to their right, tea in hand.

"What about you Matilda? What stories have we missed?" Liam gently pried.

"Well, not much. It was kind of boring without you two." Sylvia gave her a sceptical look. "Okay. Well, there was this one person in my class who was really funny."

"A person, you say?" Liam raised his eyebrows, "And what gender was this *person*?"

"Do we really have to attach labels to people, in times like this?" She argued.

"Yeah, we do. Check the dictionary." Sylvia laughed out. It was true that both *female* and *male* were defined in the dictionary, and were very specific; the term *gender* left no room for anything else.

"Fine. He's a boy."

Sylvia tore herself from Liams arms to sit straight across from Matilda. "Ooh tell me, tell me all!"

Liam rolled his eyes, "As a writer, I understand the need for gossip. Honestly, I do! But V, do you really need it when you have me," and he finished it off with an adorable smile and eyes that Sylvia ignored. She continued to bother Matilda, while Liam was just happy to see her returning to her normal spirits, and he didn't much mind hearing gossip either.

"Well, his name is Connor."

"Last name Mat! Details!"

"Okay, okay. Connor Baal."

"Okay, an arithmetic guy. Is he cute?"

"I'm going to bed!" Matilda started to stand.

"No! Mat, I'm sorry. I'll ask a different question like" Sylvia pretended to think, "is he cute?"

"Goodnight!" Matilda said over her shoulder as she left.

"Love ya!"

"You too!"

Liam rolled his eyes at the girls exchange and grabbed Sylvia by the waist, pulling her back into his arms.

"You're adorable." He told her.

"Awe, thanks. You to my love."

"I love you."

"I love you more."

"No. Same."

They spent the rest of the night watching shadows of flames dance along their arms and legs, the heat licking at their skin. A comfortable haze of warmth wrapping around them both. The fire daring to be too hot, but also not wanting to ruin the perfect scene before it. When Sylvia fell asleep, Liam carried her to their bed where he fell asleep next to her.

CHAPTER FIVE

On Wednesday morning Liam woke up with Sylvia asleep on his chest. The previous night had gone well once they got home and settled Matilda in. He tried to roll Sylvia onto her side so that he could go make breakfast, but she was a light sleeper and woke up before he even moved.

"Morning beautiful." He smiled

"Morning already?" She groaned, curling closer to Liam, smiling into his chest.

"I know, I'm sorry, but how'd you sleep?" He asked, knowing her weird sleep patterns and hoping she had slept through the night.

"Actually, pretty good, although I wouldn't mind going back!" She yawned, pulling the covers up over her.

"V, you gotta get up, we have to go to work." Liam responded, "I'm sorry." He added. "But, I'll make breakfast."

Sylvia pulled the cover down, eyes widened. "Pancakes?"

"With butter and no syrup, just like you like."

"You are literally the best person ever." Sylvia smiled.

"I know." He smiled at her over his shoulder, pulling on his shirt.

"Oh! Just remember-"

"Matilda doesn't like cheese. Got it." He finished her sentence, and Sylvia just smiled to herself. She pulled herself out of bed and put on a pair on black jeans and one of Liam's black sweaters, which was slightly big on her. She put her hair up into a messy bun, pulled on long purple socks, and pulled the sleeves on the sweater down to between her palms.

Moving the curtain aside, she walked into the small living-room kitchen combination. Liam was pouring pancake mix into a cast iron frying pan and Matilda sat across the counter from him on one of the red upholstered stools. Matilda gave her a mischievously assuming grin when she saw what Sylvia was wearing, and the brown haired girl just rolled her eyes. Liam had already laid out her favorite mug with some hot water, and Sylvia picked out a homemade peppermint tea bag, her favorite.

She curled her sleeve covered palms around the mug, "So Mat, I could close the shop for the day and we could walk around the community a bit, since it's your first official day."

"I was actually hoping to walk around by myself for a bit," Matilda shyly answered, "but I could stay around and hang with you!" She added quickly.

"No! No, that's fine. You should have some time to process everything."

"Honestly, I can stay."

"Seriously. Have fun. I have things I can get done around here anyways."

Liam shot Sylvia a look. She was a girl who couldn't handle disappointment, but she seemed to look fine. They ate their pancakes around the counter, talking and laughing, and afterwards Matilda headed off to look around the community while Liam had to leave to go to work.

He leaned against the downstairs counter. "You okay with her walking around by herself?"

"Yes. She's a grown woman, she knows the rules. But I think it's sweet that you're concerned." She added, taking a few steps towards him.

"Well, you know me. But I'm serious. I don't want anything happening to her" He added, pushing hair behind her ear.

Sylvia thought for a minute, "I used to read all these books-"

"-I know that one." He smirked.

"Ha ha ha! Very funny. But seriously, I used to read all these books, dystopian books, and there were people dying on the streets, zombies roaming around and buildings on fire. Don't get me wrong, the world we live in is messed up," she trailed off, "But, it doesn't look like it from the outside. Someone looking in might think everything is normal. So maybe since it looks normal, part of it is normal, and maybe it could be worse. Maybe because this is our new normal, it means we've gotten to a stable part of this new world."

"You just entered philosophy mode, and I love it." Liam beamed.

"I'm sorry, I don't recognize the term *philosophy.*"

"Very funny. I would tell you to look it up in the dictionary, but it's not there." Liam kissed Sylvia before walking to the door, stretching out their held hands, keeping himself connected to her as long as he could, "I have to go, but I'll be back before 6 to meet the patrolman."

"Okay." She smiled, "Goodbye, have a good day." She called out, watching the door close and looking at her empty shop.

ooo

"Mr. Wood?" A younger man knocked on Liam's door. The man was tall with short brown hair, wearing simple grey clothes. He had graduated a year after Liam.

"Silver, how many times do I have to tell you to call me Liam. C'mon in." Liam told him, waving him in. Silver approached cautiously, clutching what looked to be an old book. He sat in an oversized purple plush armchair and fiddled nervously. "So?" Liam asked expectantly.

"Oh!" Silver snapped out of his daze, "Well, I was talking to this man who was working the construction site, you know the one by 5th? Where they are redoing the top stories of that old building? They're doing a great job, very nice actually."

"Silver, I'm sorry. But where is this going?"

"Oh, right. Well I finished talking to the head of the construction team, and as I started to leave this older lady grabbed me by the arm. It was kinda creepy. I noticed that she was missing some teeth and her hair was very frizzy. She got really close to me, and her breath smelled horrible-"

"Silver."

"Right, right. She started telling me this story about a mass murderer who comes every twenty years, and Saturday is the day he's supposed to come back. I did a little digging, and I found this book. Well, it's one of the restricted books technically," Silver eyed Liam nervously, "And before you say anything, the story is really interesting, and I think it's important people hear it! Plus, news is slow this week and the story will avoid fruits and other topics you don't want to talk about. Now, I know I really shouldn't-"

"Silver, deep breath. Thanks for giving this to me," And Liam reached out for the book that Silver handed over reluctantly. "Have a great day." Liam gave him a big smile that basically said, please leave my office now. Silver fidgeted out of the chair, and right before he left Liam chimed in, "Keep up the good work."

Liam ran his hand over the cover of the brown book and opened it to the page that was bookmarked. It wasn't an old book, the publication date was exactly 20 years earlier. It was definitely a battered book, but that could be said about any Pre-Awakening literature. He ran his hand down the page and started to read;

Shots Fired At The Moon Nightclub.

Houston, Texas.

It started with a bang, and then screams rang out around the club. People scurried around, but found the doors locked. Henry B. Art gives his account of the tragedy, "My friends and I were astrophysicists at NASA before all this happened. About a week earlier, as you know, women were accepted to be astronauts. We were at the club celebrating. Everyone was so happy. There were eight of us in my booth, but there were about fifty people in the whole club. All the women were celebrating, it was an amazing accomplishment.

"I had my arm around this girl, Rosie, when suddenly there were shots. I couldn't see the shooter, but my ears blared with the sound of the bullets, like trains hitting the club. We climbed underneath the booth, and I put my arms around Rosie. She was shaking like crazy, and I suppose I was too.

"The lights were flickering, and there was screaming, so much screaming. And then suddenly, the room went silent. It was as if the the sound had been sucked out through the holes in the floors, vacuumed sealed from the room. Rosie put her hand to my mouth, and motioned to the bar, which we were right across from. It is a sight I will never forget. There was this man, but not a man, more like a boy. He was young, but muscular, with jet black hair and white skin. Those were the only things I noticed about him, partly because of the dim setting, but mostly because the rest of the scene was more prevalent. The bartender was in the clutch of this boy, a headlock, struggling to get free. Her hair was up in a ponytail, and the pencil that had been stuck behind her ear fell to the ground. Then, he put that gun to her head and he said, 'Women astrophysicists to the right. Everyone else, to the left.' and he waved his gun in the

directions. I tried to hold Rosie down, but she wouldn’t stand it. She pushed me off, tears in her eyes. She said to me, in the most honest voice I’ve ever heard, ‘Henry, you need to go. Please.’ and then she pulled herself away from me and went to stand on the right. One of my buddies had to pull me to the left. I couldn’t breathe. I didn’t want to watch, but I couldn’t tear my eyes away from that man, that boy. He threw the bartender to the left, a couple feet away from us. And then he shot every one of the women on the right. Every one of those brave, brave women. Rosie, my Rosie... I’m sorry, just give me a moment...

“The boy, before he... did what he did... said something to all of us. I’ll never forget it. He said, ‘People make decisions. It’s a factor of life. But it’s a factor of life that should have punishments. Your decisions influence people! They harm others, they have consequences for others. And none of you care! No one cares about the decisions you make, or how they affect others. Just take you all for example. You women *have all decided to risk your lives, for what? For your own dreams about what a* woman *can do! Your parents are worried about you. Your boyfriends and fiances and significant others are worried about you! And you don’t even care! You just* let *them feel that way. And for those reasons, you deserve to die.’*

"It was the most horrible thing I have ever heard in my life. Something I will never *forget for as long as I live. He just shot them, shot them all. For what reason? Just the fact that they had made a decision. If everyone was shot because they made a decision, then there would be no people left."*

Thus ends the account from Henry B. Art, someone who witnessed the first tragedy.

The shooter left the club unscathed and attacked two other locations; a convention in Washington D.C. between American scientists and the British scientists who produced the first test tube baby, and another at a dinner party for a recently appointed Supreme Court Judge in New York. (Fortunately, the judge in question escaped unharmed). In all the scenarios, the shooter left us with the same message: decisions have consequences.

Police speculate that this man, or boy as one describes, went through trauma with decisions which has caused him to go on this rampage, but besides this and the fact that he has black hair, nothing else is known about him. For this reason, police have never been able to identify the man, and he has always escaped their clutches.

The amount of killing done by this man leads people to call him a mass murder. After his last attempt in New York, a letter was sent out to newspapers across the country. No one can confirm if the letter is really from this mass murderer, although many speculate it is. Find a picture of this letter below:

I HAVE TRIED TO WARN YOU OF THE DANGERS OF DECISIONS FOR AWHILE NOW. I HOPE MY MESSAGE HAS BECOME CLEAR, AND INGRAINED IN YOUR MINDS. FOR NOW, I FEEL MY JOB IS DONE. ALTHOUGH I RESIGN MY POSITION OF TEACHER FOR NOW, KNOW THAT I WILL BE WATCHING. WILL YOU STAND MY TEST? OR WILL HUMANITY FALL BACK INTO A CYCLE OF DECISIONS- DECISIONS LEADING TO IMPACT OTHERS LIVES FOR THE WORST. I BEG YOU TO THINK ABOUT THIS EVERYONE, FOR I SPEAK THE TRUTH. REMEMBER, I WILL BE WATCHING. AND I WILL VISIT YOU AGAIN IN 20 YEARS TIME. HOPEFULLY, BY THEN, YOU HAVE COME TO CHANGE YOUR WAYS AND LIVE IN A WORLD WHERE DECISIONS DON'T HURT OR HARM.

This letter scared many people, but also assured them that they would face no more harm in 20 years. For this reason, the mass murder was given the name The *Vicennial Killer. Or, more referred to, VK, or just simply The Teacher to those who decided to follow his philosophy.*

The book continued on about The Teacher's philosophy and followers, but at this point Liam decided to stop reading. He closed the book and set it down on the desk in front of him. He tapped his fingers on his knees, suddenly feeling very small. He felt his body temperature rise and a tightening feeling in his chest. Liam wanted to publish it, he really did. It was his job as a writer to let the people know what was going on. Wasn't it? Maybe not under The House's definition. But did he really care about that? Would he have to tell Chaeronea at all?

Liam took out his electronic typewriter and started an article. He would have to word it perfectly. He tried article titles out multiple times.

Mass Murder Comes Every 20 years. No, that wouldn't work, that would get him killed. But it was the truth, wasn't it? What does that tell you about the world he lived in, Liam thought to himself. He crumpled the paper and threw it to the ground. He had to think about Sylvia, about Matilda.

Time Passes, How Have Your Decisions Affected you? Also no, too controversial. Another paper on the floor, and another, and another. Until he finally found it, the perfect wording.

Do Not Fear, It's Just a Myth.

Liam smiled to himself, a perfect way to sneak in information. A way to claim he was just trying to assure people. He was protecting them from their doubts.

"Silver!" Liam called through his open door to his layout manager, "Leave me some space on the last page!"

ooo

Sylvia said goodbye to Liam and watched him leave through the glass door. She went around the counter to sit on a stool and took off her rings, lined them up, and started putting them back on while she fiddled. Four, thin, sterling silver rings. One on her left hand ring finger, to symbolize her relationship with Liam. Two on her left hand middle finger, to show she had two others living in her house. She had gotten the second one in the mail yesterday when Matilda came to live with them. And finally, one on her right hand pinky finger; what religion she chose to follow, Christianity.

Everything Sylvia did, said, and wore was based on the rules of classification. She wasn't allowed to get her ears pierced until she had kids, one piercing per kid, and so she had had to let the holes from her childhood close up. She had to wear her hair long, she could only wear white when she was grieving, and her shop had to be open on certain hours unless she notified The House in a public manner.

Sylvia busied herself around the shop. At around noon the bell rang above her door and she found herself smiling at a younger man. He was there to deliver three dictionaries, something that happened every year after graduation. Sylvia handed over her and Liam's old ones to the man and sat down on the couch with her new version. The front was shiny and maroon, with golden lettering. "*The Dictionary*" it read. She sighed, and opened the book to the page that always mystified her the most. It read:

Female:

Synonyms: Girl, lady, women.

Definition: A long-haired human (see page 27), with the anatomy (see page 6) of a female. A human who is attracted to male humans, and can have children with and only with one other male (see page 88) through reproduction (see page 180).

A human who wears rings around her fingers. The only humans permitted to wear skirts or dresses. A female's ears may exhibit holes if and only if they have children. A human who may or may not wear eye glasses (see page 58).

Females exhibit a calm nature and practice manners around all. Females speak appropriately. Females help other humans in need.

Sylvia rolled her eyes, they had added something new this year.

Females may experience dislike towards inappropropriate items or other humans, but never show distaste or hatred towards those things.

Sylvia flipped back to another definition.

Human:

Synonyms: Person, community member.

Definition: A living being with two arms, two legs, two hands, two feet, ten fingers, ten toes, two eyes, two ears, a nose, and a form of anatomy (see page 6). Humans skin color may vary, as well as eye color. Female humans have long hair (below the shoulders), while male humans have short hair (above the shoulders).

Humans have the ability to talk, move, and jump. Humans sleep during the night, and are awake during the day. They have the ability to think and listen to instructions. They are sustained on food and water, and need daily doses of each to survive.

Humans have teeth, and need to maintain them twice a day. They also need regular bathing and hygiene regiments. Humans wear shoes and clothing to cover their bodies, stay temperature appropriate, and be respectful towards others.

Humans are attracted to the opposite sex of humans, and when the feelings becomes mutual, a "relationship" can be made. At a certain time in the relationship, two humans may decide to have sexual relations (see page 188).

Humans are mortal beings who die when:

1. Their heart stops through some natural expense of the body or

2. Harm or damage is done to the body or essential organs, causing the system to fail.

Humans live to work and fulfil their obligations to a community.

Sylvia closed her book and scoffed. She couldn't believe how hard people like her sister had worked for human rights, and then the Awakening happened and all that was gone. It was crazy for her to imagine that everything had changed because of one argument and a bomb.

ooo

Sylvia spent the rest of her day talking and helping the customers who came in; an older man with arthritis, a pregnant lady looking for some tea, and a new graduate who wanted to talk about books and had heard that Sylvia's shop was the place to go.

At around 5:30, Liam came home and Sylvia started to close up her shop.

"Matilda isn't here yet?" Liam asked

"No. She was out all day, probably just exploring."

"Seems a little dangerous for her to be-"

"Liam. Don't even finish that sentence. She is a twenty year old woman who can take care of herself." Sylvia raised her eyebrows at him.

Liam laughed, "I know, I know. But I just, I don't know, I will-"

"Always see her as that ten year old girl we met ten years ago." Sylvia finished his sentence for him. She sat on the countertop, fiddling with her sleeves, pushing spice jars around on the counter. Liam sat on the couch, his feet up on one arm. The new dictionary resting open on his lap.

"Awe, V, you finished my sentence." He smiled.

"Hey, don't flatter yourself, I'm just very observative." Sylvia shrugged and pushed away a happy Liam who got up to stand by her, all while trying to force a smile away. "Anyway, how was your day? Anything interesting happen?"

Liam's face changed, worry flashed across his eyes, but he kept his smile. No need to make Sylvia anxious. "Yeah, yeah. About that," He started.

But he was interrupted by a knock on the door. Sylvia looked at him expectantly, "Later. You should get that." She continued to look at him expectantly, but tore herself away at the second knock.

'This is a shop, don't people know they can walk right in?" She laughed, Liam following behind her.

She grabbed the brass door knob and pulled the door open, revealing a man behind the glass with dark skin and dark hair.

"William?" Sylvia gasped.

"*William?*" Liam said, "Holy. Crap."

CHAPTER SIX

Liam reached in front of Sylvia, put his full hand on the door, and closed it.

Sylvia turned to him, "You can't just close the door in his face!"

"V. That man's dead."

"Correction, I thought he was dead. He doesn't look too dead now."

"You told me you saw him crushed under a rafter next to your dead sister in the church that had a bomb dropped on it."

"Wow. Way to be sensitive Lee." Sylvia half meant.

"I'm sorry, I'm sorry." He ran a hand through his hair, "This is just so shocking. Your sister's fiance is alive." He spoke hesitantly.

"Yeah. I noticed." Sylvia smiled at him. She looked tired, confused. Memories seeping up into her facial expression. He wanted to hold her, to hug her, to help her.

But there was a knock at the door, and she opened it.

"Look. I'm really sorry, and I know this is coming as a shock to you," William started, "But if you don't let me in, your neighbors are going to get very suspicious."

"Right, of course. Come right in." And Sylvia stepped aside only for the space to be blocked by Liam.

"V, I don't know about this.

"It's alright Lee, just let him in." She gave him a look that could have moved a man from the ledge, just for wanting to do what she asked. And Liam stepped aside.

Together, they let a dead man into their house.

ooo

Matilda had never felt so free before.

She had heard about what it was like outside the walls of the school. She had even glimpsed it from on top of the roof, or in the grounds where they were permitted to play, but now she could see it up close, in real life. She could touch it and smell it and walk around it. She felt like when she was younger and her mother gave her too much sugar, hyped, surreally aware of the world around her.

She loved Sylvia, she truly did. But she was in a mood where she just had to explore by herself. She didn't want to talk or know the facts of the town. She wanted to breathe in the cold air that hurt her lungs. She wanted to run down the completely silent streetways and hear the sound of her footsteps on the dark pavement. She wanted to climb up a firescape and sit, watching the clouds roll over the sky.

And that's exactly what she did.

Matilda looked up at the street signs and turned left. She wrapped her purple scarf around her neck as she walked down the street that she assumed was a residential neighborhood. Matilda walked past piles of reddish brown bricks, chipped on the edges and corners, piled in small batches. There were square stacks of them along each side of the road, and in the middle of the road, for there was nothing that travelled along the road that bricks might cause harm to. Third stories of houses had been left in their destructive state after the Awakening, with half and quarter walls still up. Chairs could be visible on these stories; bedrooms and living quarters converted into rooftop lounges. The bricks stayed on the road, heavy reminders that something had happened here, happened everywhere, and there was no place to go.

When Matilda got to the 18th house on the road, she strolled up the stairs to the doorway and knocked, not bothering to fix her windblown hair. She hadn't told Liam or Sylvia where she was headed today, but they hadn't asked. She honestly didn't mind telling them about him, she really didn't, but she got so flustered at the cheesy questions of the relationship and just thought that not telling them every detail would keep some of her privacy.

She really didn't mind telling them about him though, she wanted to. She wanted to talk about how happy she was.

She rolled her eyes at how sappy she was becoming.

The black door opened to a happy face, Connor. He grabbed her in a hug.

"Hey! How have you been? How's the house?" He asked her.

"It's so nice! And totally not weird or anything because I've known them for so long. They're so nice, and I get to see them everyday now, just like when we were in school together. They've been asking about you." She smiled at him as he led her inside, sitting down on the couch and handing her some tea. They sat across from each other on the couch, not touching. They hadn't been as rebellious as Sylvia and Liam in school, and weren't quite used to showing affection yet. "But what about you? How are you doing with these strangers? It looks like a nice house." She said, looking around.

"Yeah. I've been good, honestly." He looked down at her, "They are definitely strangers though. This morning we ate breakfast together and then bam, they were out the door. But it's all good, I've had the place all to myself, and now you're here, and that makes everything better." He smiled, and she moved his short brown hair out of his eyes.

"Well, after the three months we can move in together, and you won't have to live with strangers."

"Totally. I'm just worried because we live on opposite sides of the town. You better visit me!"

"You better visit me!"

"Well, fine then! Looks like you've got yourself a deal!"

"Fine!"

"Fine!"

And they both burst out laughing.

ooo

Liam and Sylvia sat on the couch together across from the blue armchair that William occupied.

"So." He started.

"So," Liam glared.

"So." Sylvia sighed.

William's eyes glanced around the shop before focusing on a spot by his feet. "Okay, I guess I'll start." And Sylvia nodded her head in agreement. "This is weird, really weird. I get that. I get that you're probably upset, and that this brings up weird stuff for you. And that's understandable. I think we should talk and go through all those... weird things. But not now. I have people who are expecting me at their houses. Let's make a time to talk and I will explain all that weird stuff."

"Wow." Liam started, "And the award for the most times *weird* was ever used in a sentence goes to-"

"Liam." Sylvia pleaded, "Let's just do it." She turned to William, "When can you come back?"

"Friday. I have a few hours off in the middle of the day. Everyone will be at work, it's the perfect time. We can meet here?" Liam stood up and walked to the back of the store. Sylvia's eyes followed him, she didn't want him to be mad at her, but this was right. It was right to have William explain himself. The pros outweigh the cons, and that's how Sylvia made all her decisions. She went to answer him but Liam cut in.

"Look William," Liam started, "We've never met before, but let's get one thing straight."

Sylvia took a deep breath. Her thoughts were rushing and she needed air. She needed Liam to be near her and she needed William to get out.

"That's fine!" She suddenly burst out, exhaling her breath. "Tomorrow. Now can you just go? Matilda will be home soon."

William stood up and started to say something, but when he caught Liam's eye he shut his mouth. He left and the door jingled behind him.

"I'm sorry." Sylvia started, and suddenly Liam was next to her, holding her. He set the things that made him upset aside and put her first.

He held her, but after a minute he had to say something, "V, don't get mad, but we don't know if that man is even William. He could just be pretending to get something from you" And suddenly Sylvia was stiff in his arms.

"It's him, okay? I know it is. I wouldn't forget him. I *can't* forget him." She moved to the countertop and lifted herself up to sit on the counter with her hands in her lap, hair dangling in front of her eyes. Liam ran a hand through his hair.

Matilda walked through the door, "Hey everyone! Sorry I'm late." But sensing the pressure in the room she closed her mouth, stopping in the middle of the room.

"Matilda, could you give us a second?" Liam asked, while Sylvia shook her head and looked out through the window, her arms crossed over her chest. Matilda slowly nodded and left to go upstairs.

Liam turned towards Sylvia, trying to be rational. "You thought he was dead Sylvia. Dead. And dead people just don't show up at your front door!" Liam got more angry at himself as he went on, letting his emotions swill into the words.

"Really!? I just thought after you died, you carried on with your life with a giant sign hung from your neck saying 'Dead'!" Sylvia flung her hands up.

"Ugh, that's not the point!" Liam came to stand in front of her, "It's creepy! We don't know what he's capable of, where's he been the past 10 years!"

"Well, I'm sorry if my sister's fiance is creepy to you!" She moved off the counter around Liam, standing with her hands on her hips.

"V, c'mon that's not what I meant." He shot her an apologizing look, "But we don't know anything about him. How can you just let him in here?"

"I want answers Lee! He's going to give them to me, he knows what happened!"

"You're so damn stubborn sometimes." Liam said, and then he realized his mistake. Sylvia became drawn back, hurt flashed in her eyes. It was quick, it was subtle. Only Liam would have noticed. Matilda, who was perched on the staircase, unseen, didn't even realize what had just happened. She only took in the yelling.

"Excuse me for trying to figure out our crazy, stupid world!" Sylvia shot back.

Liam hated himself before he even spoke, "And if you actually lived in the real world with us, instead of your imagination, you would realize how dangerous this is! Look, Sylvia," Liam said, realizing this conversation was hurting her, that this wasn't the way to talk about this. He slowed his pace and retracted the volume "I just don't want you to get hurt, or end up blaming yourself for something that wasn't your fault."

But Sylvia was already too deep in, "I can take care of myself." She met his eyes, her words burning him. Liam let his hurt fuel his anger, his protectiveness being used against him.

"Right! Oh I'm sorry, I forgot! We have the strong, capable Sylvia Blue with us today! Let me just ask, where were you the day a bomb dropped on your sister's wedding?"

Sylvia kept her eyes glued to his, as the mad gleam faded out of him. She grabbed her coat off the couch and left. The door signaling her exit.

"V, wait."

But she was already gone.

Liam sunk down to the ground and punched the hardwood floor. Why did he say that? How did those words reach his mouth? When he closed his eyes, he was met with the mean face of his worst enemy; Anger, protectiveness, smiling back at him, winning again.

Sylvia pulled her coat on, tears forming in her eyes through anger. A background of fear, shaking, and nervousness settled in her bones. She couldn't breathe right, she couldn't walk straight and her head was dizzy with the weight of thoughts. She shoved her hands in her pockets and ducked her head, putting one foot in front of the other. She didn't know where she was going, she didn't care.

She only wished Liam was with her.

Sylvia shoved her hands in her pockets and made aimless turns; with a clear head she would know exactly where she was going, but right now she wasn't thinking. She realized very quickly she wasn't wearing shoes, only thick wool socks that had been very comfortable in her store but became very cold as she swept down the sidewalk.

She came to a small square park where the grass was slowly starting to turn towards the grey scale, beginning to get frosty on the tips. She sat down on a long wooden bench that chilled her skin through the thin cloth of her clothing and she tilted her head up to watch the landscape. Birds sat on trees while people walked the streets, unnoticed by Syvlia. Silence surrounded her and a breeze made her bare face cold. She sat while strange memories of her sister came back to her.

ooo

"Find Sylvia a boyfriend." Wallace said.

"No."

"But Sylvia!"

"No! That's not going on the list." Sylvia insisted.

"Fine!" Wallace tried to think of a new thing, "Have a fashion show." Sylvia nodded her head and picked up a red marker, writing what her sister said in big block letters on the paper, with a check box before. They were making a basket list, instead of a bucket list, for the next summer.

"What else?"

"Make bubble tea."

"Make bubble tea? How are we going to do that?" Sylvia asked, while picking a blue marker and writing it in curvy letters.

"I don't know, but we'll figure it out."

They went on with their basket list for a couple hours, writing all over the page upside down and sideways until the page was finished. They threw markers at each other, jumped on the bed, and ate sugary snacks. Wallace took everything down from her bulletin board and hung the paper on the wall.

Sylvia and her took lots of pictures and then fell on the bed in a heap.

"Wallace?" She started, "Are you sure you want to do all this stuff with me?"

"What do you mean?"

"Well, I'm your little sister. Isn't that kind of, I don't know, uncool?"

"Totally not. You're super cool."

"Then why do you call me a brat half the time?"

"Cause you can be annoying."

"But then if I'm annoying why don't you do this with someone who isn't annoying?"

"Sylvia," Wallace sighed, "Would you stop trying to poke holes in this? It's going to be fun, you and I are going to have fun, okay? Now pass the M&M's." So Sylvia passed the bowl to her sister. Wallace ate most of the candy, while giving the orange ones to Sylvia because Sylvia only liked to eat the orange ones.

Sylvia continued to wonder why her sister didn't want to hang out with her friends. But it became clear later on that Wallace didn't have a ton of people to hang out with in the summer. It made Sylvia sad, but also happy because she got to be Wallace's favorite.

ooo

Sylvia leaned forward and put her elbows on her knees, her head in her hands. She couldn't breath.

ooo

"Move over to the left."

"Why?"

"There is a cool ray of light over there."

"Oh, okay. Is this good?"

"Totally! This one's so good, come see!"

Sylvia hiked the fabric of her dress up higher to move out of the river. When she got to the beach her bare feet started to feel the hard curves of the rocks, and she let the fabric of her dress fall on her wet legs. Wallace held a camera, and on the screen there was a picture of Sylvia in her blue dress with the white flowers. The layers of fabric were curled up in her hands to keep them out of the river she was standing in. A ray of light fell down across her face down to the rocks below her.

"Wow Wallace. That's a really great shot."

"Yeah. You look great in it."

"Ha, I only look good because of you. My hair's a mess and I'm slouching."

"You look nice, you always do."

"Thank you."

"But... you're about to look a whole lot wetter!"

"What? Wallace! Don't you dare..."

But suddenly she was dripping wet and her sister innocently held an empty bucket of water. Sylvia glared at her, and Wallace put her camera down while Sylvia proceeded to push her into the river. They fought, splashed, and ran through the water. Later on they sat on the riverbed drying out, and then they caught crayfish from beneath the rocks.

"Crayfish are the cousins of lobsters." Sylvia started, after she had put another one in the bucket.

"Don't lobsters mate for life?"

"I don't know. But if they do, does that mean crayfish do too?"

"Why would they? They aren't the same animal."

"But they're related. Don't related species do similar things?"

"I guess. But it's not like they were raised together."

"Huh. Maybe they just learn from each other." Sylvia looked up at her older sister, crouched next to her in the river.

"Maybe they do."

ooo

She started to cry, and her tears turned to anger.

But I saw her dead. I saw them *dead. What if I abandoned her? None of this was ever supposed to happen.*

Sylvia saw her whole life in front of her. She saw everything Wallace should have been doing with her. She saw Liam, the love of her life, and wondered for the millionth time what her sister would have thought of him, if they would get along.

Her whole body shook and tears fell down her face and hit the ground before her. She cried for all the scenarios she had made up in her head that would never come true. She cried for the sister she had lost, and the life Wallace would never have.

She stood up and paced in front of the bench, wrapping her arms around herself. She needed to take a breath. She needed to remember that Wallace was dead. She needed to convince herself that William hadn't just turned her world upside down. She needed to start living in reality.

"Just breathe Sylvia," She muttered to herself.

CHAPTER SEVEN

Matilda slowly crept down the stairs as Liam shrank down to the floor, remembering when she had first met Liam. She had been Sylvia's friends first, before he even came along. When he did, it took some time for them to get used to each other. Matilda had a way of voicing her opinions, even unpopular ones, while Liam took the approach that all opinions were valid and none of them should be undermined by the other. Sylvia didn't ever choose between the two of them, and eventually they got along.

Matilda walked up to Liam and put her hand on his shoulder, very unused to physical contact between them. She kneeled down to his right side, keeping her hand in place, and just sat there for a bit.

Liam silently cried while Matilda rested her head on his shoulder, her way of offering support to him.

When he calmed down, he started the conversation, "I feel horrible. What I said was horrible. I'm horrible." He choked out.

"Liam. No you are not, everyone says things they don't mean to say." Matilda started.

"But Sylvia doesn't! She has never..."

"That's because she apologizes for *everything*. And Sylvia rants a lot, she definitely has those feelings, it's just not something she expresses to the specific person she has them towards. You know what I mean?"

"Yeah, I know. I wish I could be more like her."

"You wanna have her temper?" Matilda laughed.

"I already have a temper!"

"That's why you're perfect for each other." Matilda smiled.

Liam chuckled, "You just proved your point in a very roundabout way."

"What can I say? You came to it all by yourself." She smiled.

They stayed silent for a little while, "I'm going to find her."

"Liam. She'll be back. You don't have to go after her." But Liam had already moved himself from her embrace, grabbed two sets of gloves and scarves and left through the front door.

He turned left and strode down the road before stopping and turning to figure out where Sylvia was. He decided to go to all her favorites.

He started with the balcony of the old abandoned library, and then the roof of the newspaper building. He looked at the deli a few blocks from their apartment, with the old man who loved Sylvia. He walked down to the river to check the pier, where she loved to sit and read. But he prayed she wasn't there because of the cold temperature and strong wind. When he rounded the corner and didn't see her sitting on the concrete he let out a sigh of relief, but panic flushed his cheeks and he racked his brain for other options. He walked to the small park a few streets behind their apartment but couldn't find her there either. He sat down on a bench and took a few deep breaths. He was getting worried, especially since she wasn't wearing good clothing for the cold temperature.

Liam stood up from the bench and turned to go back home. When he got to the spice shop he turned the knob to find Sylvia sitting criss cross on the floor of her shop, trying to take off her coat.

When he first walked in, she tried to pretend he wasn't there. She kept her head down and fiddled with her buttons, but was having trouble because of her freezing hands. Liam tried to smile. He knew she blamed herself for the fight, without good reason. He also knew her hands were freezing and he instantly felt bad. So he put down the gloves he was holding and went over to her, undoing her coat for her.

"Here." And he took off her coat, wrapping a scarf around her freezing face.

"Thanks," she smiled sheepishly, meeting his eyes for a brief second, but Liam stayed standing where he was.

"V I want to say,"

Sylvia cut him off, "No Lee, you were right."

"Don't you dare. I was absolutely not right."

"No seriously, I'm sorry."

"Sylvia! Would you just shut up and let me apologize?" He grabbed both her hands in his, her gaze hit the floor.

"I was horrible. That fight was horrible, and what I said was not forgivable. I shouldn't have said it or doubted you in any way. I trust you Sylvia. I trust your decisions and the way you feel about people. And even if I thought you were wrong about this, I shouldn't have acted like I did. I thought I was trying to protect you by fighting you on this, but I know you can take care of yourself. Honestly, I do. I want us to be a team, not just me making decisions for us."

"Lee, I know. I know all that." And she leaned into him, "But I do need you. And I'm really, really sorry."

"Stop apologizing for things you didn't do."

"But I apologize for everything." She smiled shyly.

"Not for this. I love you Sylvia Blue. And I trust you completely. I'm with you completely"

Sylvia smiled, "Same to you. I accept your apology."

Liam led Sylvia upstairs and left her in front of the fire while he made dinner. No matter how much they struggled together, learned together, and fought together, everything always seemed to turn out alright. Liam honestly thought it was sappy, but at the same time he liked being so stable in a relationship. She would always forgive him because she truly loved him, no matter how stupid it sounded. And Liam hoped there would never be a fight when he felt like he didn't have to apologize.

Because if he didn't apologize, would she still forgive him?

Every bone in his body said of course she will. But at the same time, if it was the other way, if it was someone else, someone who was not Sylvia, would he forgive them, even without an apology?

ooo

Sylvia woke up early in the morning and rolled over to a note on her pillow.

I am SO SO SORRY about yesterday. Went out early to take care of something, didn't want to wake you. See you before William comes. Love, Wood.

Sylvia smiled to herself as she brought the note to a small box she kept under her bed, and then stashed the box so Liam wouldn't know she kept his notes. She stared up at the ceiling from her bed. She had truly forgiven Liam; she was that person who forgave people because she knew they really meant their apology. She knew Liam had meant what he said, and he also knew he was beating himself up over their fight. So she decided to do something for him, just to show him that he was completely forgiven.

"Mat! Mat! MATILDA! Wake up!"

Matilda practically fell through the curtain of her room into the living room. She wore gray sweatpants and a red shirt and her hair was flung into a messy bun with her glasses at a crooked angle.

"I'm here! I'm here. It's okay, it's all good, what do you need?" Matilda said out of breath.

"Breakfast! We have to make breakfast before Liam gets home." Sylvia said, grabbing pans and jars and food from the vintage refrigerator.

"*That's* what you woke me up for? Breakfast?"

Sylvia halted. Moving to look at Matilda, she blinked, "Yes."

Matilda sighed and adjusted her glasses. "Okay. Well, you can't make pancakes. The outside will be black and the inside will be raw, I'll do it. You just cook the bacon."

ooo

When the clock read 3am Liam snuck out. The paper had been out for an hour by then and he knew she would already be reading it.

If he thought it was cold during the day, the night topped the icy smile of the wind with a firm cold glare. He had dressed in nice clothes and topped it with a black coat, scarf, and gloves. He wanted to be invisible, he didn't want any attention.

He felt very invigorated by what he was doing, but also terrified. He had always had a curfew, whether it was at school or before the Awakening at his house with his mom. He had come to like it that way. He liked being inside, whether he was awake or not. He liked the security of the walls around him with the engulfing dark swirling outside it. He usually never went outside past midnight. This was new, this was different; and turns out he was having fun.

He strode through the cold air feeling hints of freedom and danger. He walked faster and realized he was on an unfamiliar road. Suddenly, he felt overwhelmed, and his thoughts started to wander;

what would happen if someone caught me? He steadied himself by taking a deep breath. The cold around him made him feel small, and all he wanted was to go back indoors in the warmth where he didn't feel so small. He forced himself to just keep walking until he took the appropriate turns and finally found his way in front of a white door.

When he sat down, the panic broke around him.

He rested his arms on his knees, staring at the ground below him. He had found his way, but he didn't want to look up, because if he did there would be too much space before him. Too much room that anything could fill.

He was twenty six and still afraid of the dark.

He closed his eyes and took a deep breath. He didn't want her to see his panic attack. He didn't want her to see the worry that was knocking on his head and threatening to leak through his ears and eyes. He thought of Sylvia, took a deep breath, and rose off the cold stone steps to knock on Chaeronea's door.

A few moments later Chaeronea stood in the doorway of her house wearing black shorts and a purple tank top. Liam was caught completely off guard by her appearance.

"Of course. It's you." She sighed, "Go away." And Chaeronea started to close the door on him, but he snapped back into reality in time to put his foot inside of the door.

"Chaeronea! Please. I know you are pissed at me, but I need to talk to you. It's really important. Please just let me in and you can yell all you want."

The pressure on the other side of the door continued for a couple seconds until finally Chaeronea backed off and led Liam inside, walking at a brisk pace.

Chaeronea's apartment was barely decorated, with gray walls and a few bowls of fruit. The lights were bright and all her flat surfaces were covered in papers that when Liam tried to look at, she pushed aside.

She motioned for Liam to sit on her beige couch, but when he did she remained standing. The paper was open next to him on the cushion.

"Look, Chaeronea."

"No. You don't talk. I talk, you listen." She started to pace in front of him, "That article. That article! That *article.*" She whispered angrily.

"What article?" Liam tried to play dumb, lightening the mood.

"I said no talking!" Liam folded his hands in his lap, "That article was *not* approved by me, or the

Reining Powers. And you know that! That article is going to get me fired, or worse! And I'm taking you down with me, you hear? This is your fault! What were you *thinking*? A myth about some crazy teenager who runs around killing crowds? What did you expect to happen? Huh?" She sighed, pausing briefly, "Tomorrow you and I are going to explain this to the community board. Yeah, that's right, *the community board*. We are going to say how very sorry we are and how we don't know what happened to us. We are going to say how we must have gone crazy! Had a blow to our heads! We will get down on our knees if we have to and..."

"...And that all sounds great. Seriously, it does," Liam stood up and grabbed Chaeronea's arms, "But, I can't tomorrow." He said hesitantly, "It's why I came to talk to you. I need you to cover for me, I can't make it to work."

Chaeronea threw his hands off her.

"What?!"

"I know. I know it's bad. But Sylvia-"

"What? Sylvia fell down and twisted her ankle and needs you home? Or did she accidentally mix herbs into the wrong bowl and get herself high? You realize I don't actually work for the newspaper, right? I am this community's communication *director*. That's a big deal. I talk at important events, I make sure people hear what the Reining Powers want them to hear, I am trusted by them! And what does Sylvia do? Mix spices? Talk about books?"

"Learn that her sister's dead fiance is actually alive."

"Wha-what?" Chaeronea stopped pacing as she grasped for words. Finally, she sat on the couch and Liam took the spot next to her.

"When the Awakening happened, Sylvia was in a church, at her sister's wedding." Liam started.

"Oh."

"She watched her sister die, and her sister's fiance die."

"Oh."

"And it's really dangerous for me to be telling you this. Especially because of your status in the community. But it turns out, he wasn't dead. He *just* reconnected with Sylvia, and they are meeting tomorrow. Well, I guess it's today if you look at the time. And Chaeronea, I know it's horrible timing. I really, really do. But I need to be there for her. I'm sorry."

They sat in silence for a minute, "Oh." Chaeronea said.

"Chaeronea, again I'm so sorry and I know you want to kill me-"

"Go. Go be with Sylvia today, she needs you."

"Chaeronea please, I'm begging," he paused for a moment "wait. What?" Liam stopped short.

Chaeronea sat stone still, her gaze pointed ahead, past Liam's head. "My dad was abusive all my life. One day, he went out for groceries and he never came back. That was the day of the Awakening. I assumed he had died out there, like most people did. Then one day in school, during my Reporting for the Community class, we had to watch a trial and write a paper on it. It was a trial for a secret underground group of people who were trying to rise up in the early days of The House. Only a select group of us were allowed to watch, allowed to know it even existed."

"Sylvia told me about that, she had heard rumors." Liam offered, trying to find a middle ground.

"Yes." Chaeronea nodded, "Rumors circulated about who the people were, where they were from, all the different details. I was so excited to be a part of that select group, but then I saw him. My dad was one of the people on trial.

"I don't care what people whisper about The House or the Reining Powers. My dad was a horrible, mean man. And they punished him, and I am forever thankful for that."

"Why are you telling me this?"

Chaeronea met Liam's gaze. "Because, no matter what happens - no matter what you tell yourself - whether you understand the truth or you know they got what they deserved; It's a horrible feeling when dead men come back to life."

CHAPTER EIGHT

"Pancakes?"

"Spiced pancakes."

"You made pancakes?"

"Well, technically I made the batter. Matilda cooked them."

"That makes more sense." Liam chuckled.

"Hey! I could make pancakes if I wanted to!" Sylvia protested.

"But we don't want you to," Matilda laughed, "I'll grab the jam for the pancake stacks."

Liam pulled Sylvia off to the side. "What's all this for?"

"My way of saying sorry," she smiled.

"But you don't need to be sorry!" He insisted.

"Well, neither do you! So can't we just enjoy our pancakes?" She smiled.

"Yes, we absolutely can. But, before that, how are you feeling?" He asked, gently rubbing her arm.

"Oh, well, you know." Sylvia shrugged, hanging her head. Liam tucked her hair behind her hair, a familiar and welcomed move. Sylvia raised her eyes to meet his gaze. "I've seen a ghost." She answered honestly, and Liam pulled her into his arms.

"Hey, I got the newspaper!" Matilda said from the kitchen, and Sylvia pulled back, smiling at Liam. Sylvia intertwined their hands and walked them back to the room Matilda was in, happily grabbing the newspaper from Matilda.

"We can save that for later." Liam said, snatching it from Sylvia.

"But I like reading your articles. Didn't you say you had a story you were really excited about at work?"

"Yes I did. But you can read it later," and he held the paper above him as Sylvia tried to reach it.

"Lee! Just give me the paper!" She said, refusing to jump for it, "Matilda! Help me out here!"

"Sorry V, but I don't know if I should get in the middle of this." She smirked.

"Sylvia, you spent all this time on these nice warm pancakes. Can we just enjoy them and leave the monotony of scripted news afterwards?" Liam asked. Sylvia gave in, she was hungry.

"Alright, but I'm reading it afterwards."

They all sat down to breakfast but Sylvia was still curious why Liam was hiding the paper from her, and she kept sneaking glances at him, even while Matilda talked right at her. Her thoughts wandered, but at the same time, she had so much on her mind, she didn't know what to focus on more. After a while, she decided to relax the best she could.

"Do you need help finding your work?" Liam asked Matilda.

"I've got the address, I'll be fine."

"Your job is so cool. 'Relay'. You get to talk to other communities. *Other communities.* Wow." Sylvia chimed in.

"It is pretty cool, although I've heard it might be kind of boring. It's not like we're sharing gossip, or even coordinates. Just ration numbers and climate stuff I think."

"Well, I'm sure you'll have some fun."

"Yeah, and it's a job, so that's good."

"Everyone has a job." Liam added from the kitchen sink.

"Or, you could say that a job has everyone." Sylvia smiled up at him.

"That makes no sense," he countered.

"It does if you think about it."

"No it doesn't."

"Yes it does."

"No it really-"

"Hey, where did Matilda go?"

ooo

Matilda shouldered her bag as she left through the shop's front door. She stared at the paper in front of her and tried to find the right street to go down. She told Liam she knew where she was going but she honestly had no idea. She didn't tell Liam because now she was depending on them for everything; food, clothes, a place to stay. She just wanted to try and do this one thing on her own.

She made a turn and continued down the street. She looked around at the street signs and the numbers on the buildings but could not find her way around the community she didn't know. Finally, not wanting to be late, she decided to ask for directions. A tall man with white hair and black glasses was leaning against the wall of a building, reading the paper.

"Excuse me. Sir?"

He looked startled, "Oh, um, yes?"

"I was wondering if you could give me directions to the Relay Office?"

"Right. You must be a new graduate. Well, it's down that street. Take two rights and you'll be right in front of it. Who are you staying with? Why didn't they tell you?"

"Oh, I'm staying with Sylvia Blue and Liam Wood, and well I just didn't-"

The man suddenly moved off the wall, "I have to go. It was nice to meet you." And he left down the street in the opposite direction.

"Oh. Well, it was nice meeting you as well." She called after him, realizing very quickly they had never actually exchanged names.

When Matilda got to her new office she walked right in because of the cold weather and bumped into a tall, black haired woman.

"Oh, I'm sorry!" Matilda started.

Chaeronea barely glanced at her before she started talking, "You must be Matilda, the new graduate. I'm Chaeronea, Director of Communications in this community. My office is right upstairs, but you'll be working down here at this desk." Chaeronea, the black haired lady said, whisking Matilda through the office. "Here's the phone to connect you to other communities. I hope I don't have to explain what you'll be doing here."

"No ma'am, I know what Relay people do and I'm honored-"

"Great. Well here is a list of communities you will be in touch with as well as their extensions. This sheet is the generic sheet for what information you need to get from these communities. You can copy them over there." Chaeronea handed Matilda a black, empty notebook for what she assumed was the copying, and a thick green booklet, "You can start by reading this book. It's the rules of this job and this is a very serious job, mind you. There are certain procedures and eddictue to follow. I have to go, I have things to take care of, not that that's any of your business, but if you have questions ask Neil or Sarah." She pointed to two people hunched over desks, "You should have plenty to do today. Who are you living with?" Chaeronea asked Matilda off guard.

"Oh um, Sylvia Blue and Liam-"

"Wood." Chaeronea said thoughtfully, taking a minute to actually look at Matilda for the first time since she had walked into the room. Their eyes met. "It figures. Well, I have to go." Chaeronea explained, talking more to herself.

Chaeronea grabbed her coat and left through the front door. Matilda didn't want to call her new boss rude or unprofessional, but she was confused by their first meeting. She decided to get to know her before making a decision.

Matilda sat down at her desk and opened the green booklet.

Chapter One: Communication Between The Communities; Etiquette.

Matilda sighed, it was going to be a long day.

ooo

Liam was in the shower and Sylvia stood in front of the mirror. She put her hair up and took it down again. She tried brushing it out but it wouldn't stay straight. She put it up again, but small little curls escaped her ribbon of fabric and threw themselves away from her head. She sighed and decided to braid it in two pieces down each side of her head.

Sylvia walked out of the bathroom to the living room where she found the paper on the countertop. She sighed again. She wanted to pick the paper up and read his article. He wouldn't mind, would he? He always liked when she read his pieces. He was just joking this morning.

Right?

That's what she told herself when she picked up the paper and scanned the pages for Liam's byline. She found it at the very end of the paper, last page, the title reading *Do Not Fear, It's Just a Myth*. Sylvia smiled at his way with words and kept reading. She read about the first shooting. About the second and third shootings. She read about The Teacher and she read about the prophecy. Although she had to admit Liam framed it very well, her heart started to race. She felt pressure in her head and a tingling in her fingers. They would kill for this.

They would kill *him* for this.

It echoed through her head. It wasn't even a question, just a simple six word statement that made her head pound.

William was alive and Liam was going to die; that's what Sylvia was thinking about the moment Liam came out of the bathroom wearing a towel around his waist. He saw her holding the paper and stopped in his tracks, running a hand through his damp hair.

"You're mad." He started.

"No."

"You're worried."

"No..."

"Sylvia."

"Well, yeah. To be honest I'm really worried, Lee." Liam sat down next to Sylvia.

"I didn't mean to worry you." He said honestly, softly.

"But I am! Okay? I'm worried because I love you." She stood up and started pacing, newspaper flailing in her hands, "I'm worried because we live in a world where this isn't allowed. I'm worried because you have people who love you and who care about you and not everyone has that! And you could be taken away from us."

"Hey, hey." Liam stood up and grabbed her wrists, "I'm not going anywhere, you hear me? I've already talked to Chaeronea about this." And just like that, Sylvia burst out laughing. She was laughing so hard that she couldn't stand, and she collapsed on the couch. "What's, what's so funny, V?" He asked, starting to smile.

"For-for-forget about th-the Reining Pow-wers. Chae-ronea i-is going to *kill* you-u-u!" Sylvia said through laughter. Liam grabbed her ankles and swung her curled up body onto his lap.

He let her laugh for a minute before saying, "Sylvia, I really don't want you to be mad at me."

"Liam," Sylvia breathed out, calming down, "You're an old-fashioned-write-for-the-people kind of guy. Sometimes, it gets you into this. But I understand it, and I love it. I'm right here supporting you, after the initial panic attack and questions."

"You haven't asked any." Liam smiled at her, lacing together their fingers.

"Well, first, go change." She said looking down at the towel he was still wearing, "And then, get comfortable."

○○○

Chaeronea folded her hands over the long wooden table in front of her. She had called this meeting because she thought it was the best way to get ahead of the problem. She wore her best business suit. Black pants and jacket, white undershirt. Her hair was up in a tight bun. She looked straight ahead, staying still.

The important people of the community rustled in and took their places at the table. She recognized some big shots, a couple Reining Powers, and some people smaller in stature like herself. When they had taken their seats and rustled the papers in front of them accordingly, they all turned to her at the same time.

Don't show fear.

"Well I guess we should start, since it looks like everyone is here." Everyone around the table nodded. "Community leaders, I have called you all here to talk about today's newspaper. Specifically, the article titled *Do Not Fear, It's Just a Myth.*"

Silence.

"I disgustingly admit that I was unaware this article was being published. And had I known, I assure you I would have taken the appropriate steps to get it out of the paper. Unfortunately, this mistake was made, and the article is out there."

Chaeronea made sure to make eye contact with each member of the table while she spoke.

"With that said, Liam Wood, the writer of this article and editor of the paper, is very esteemed with a great reputation. This is the first time something like this has ever happened. I have already talked with him, and I can promise that nothing like this will ever happen again. I would like to plead mercy on this man, who is in a healthy, House approved relationship, with a graduate living with him. He has been in charge of the paper for many years, and has always done and published what we've asked. It would be a shame to lose him. I personally would like to take full responsibility for what has happened, and therefore, here is what I propose to fix this matter. I'll make an announcement at the community meeting to confirm what was said in the article. That way, it looks like it was 100% approved by us. After that, no more mention of it will be made. We can all forget this experience and not worry anyone else. Thoughts?"

Chaeronea took a deep breath. Chairman Clementine's second in command was at the table, John Alberstien. Chaeronea didn't know him personally but she knew of the power he held. He spoke with a firm voice, "That sounds fine, meeting adjourned. Get on with your day everyone."

People stood up to leave, slowly, shocked. Chaeronea was surprised she had gotten out of the situation so easily. She knew she was a good speaker, all her teachers had told her so back in school, but she didn't expect it to work so well on a group of highly educated, powerful people. Her hands slightly shook as she grabbed the papers in front of her, waiting for the room to clear.

"Chaeronea?" Clementine's second in charge spoke.

She turned to meet his gaze, her mouth went dry, "Yes?"

"Chairman Clementine would like to see you and talk privately."

"Oh. Oh, yes, of course." She stuttered, sounding highly unlike herself, "When?" She had never met Chairman Clementine before, and she tried to think of someone she personally knew who had.

"Would now work for you?" John asked, although it did not seem like a question

"Certainly." She hoped her voice didn't shake.

"Right this way."

Damn you, Liam. She thought, and was led out of the conference room..

ooo

"Well, do you believe in it?" Sylvia asked him.

"Believe that a man who killed people for making decisions twenty years ago is coming back? No way. Maybe if the Awakening never happened. But in this kind of world, you'd have to be crazy to pull something like that." Liam shot a paper airplane across the shop.

"But, isn't he crazy? He did it in the first place."

"True. But the Awakening changed people. He'd have to have survived the wars and gone through The Houses school and stuff like that. I bet even if he is alive, the Awakening knocked the crazy out of him."

"Well if you don't believe in it, why'd you write about it?"

Liam thought for a moment, "Because if there is a small chance it's true, people deserve to know and they deserve to be warned. So they can be prepared and such."

Sylvia nodded, "I wonder if we could find him in the records."

"We don't know much about him. And it's not like his file would read *Teenage Mass Murderer.*"

"Well I know that. But it would be like detective work. They must have found his identity, he would have been revealed in the lie detector tests. "

"You read too many books." Liam smiled.

"I don't have enough books."

Knock. Knock. Knock.

Sylvia put down the paper airplane she was making.

"I think that's him." Liam eased in.

"Right. Yeah, that's probably him. Why is he knocking? Why doesn't he just come in?" Sylvia said, her voice laced with nerves that turned into a dull anger.

"We don't have to do this if you're uncomfortable." Liam reassured.

"No, it's fine. This is my shop and I can throw him out if I want to. Plus," She paused, "you're here." She said softly, smiling up at him.

"Yes I am. Right here next to you." Liam told her, walking to stand by Sylvia. They linked hands and she reached for the door knob.

"Okay. The first thing you need to know is that this is a shop. The sign says OPEN and I know you can read, so read it and get the message that you can just walk right in." Sylvia started immediately while motioning for William to enter.

William looked around the shop, "Oh, I just thought you were going to close up today because we were meeting."

Sylvia rolled her eyes, "You're the one who didn't want to be suspicious. If someone comes in, I'll help them and they'll leave. It's Friday anyway." She was standing behind the counter making tea. She felt very wound up, a little angry. She was nervous and her energy was up high so she was snapping a bit when she talked. Liam tried a short conversation with William and put his hand over hers on the countertop. Something very small, but something that showed he was there with her. She liked it, she took a deep breath and let her steam out. She was going to act calm and collected today.

William fidgeted standing near the front door after only taking a few small steps into the building. He watched Liam next to Sylvia and felt like he was intruding, not only on a couple, but a whole life he had missed. A whole life he had removed himself from.

Sylvia brought tea out and they sat in the same positions as the day before. Sylvia stared at her sister's fiance and Liam kept his gaze slightly above William's head.

"So, where should I start?" William asked.

"The beginning would be nice," said Sylvia.

"Right. What do you want to know?"

"Everything." Sylvia's tone was flat.

"Right, of course." William nodded, wringing his hands together. The tea before them sat untouched.

"What's your last name?" Liam cut in, his tone sharp. He was there to be supportive to Sylvia, but she didn't have to cut this man any slack. According to him, William was dead.

"Diving right in I see." William tried a smile to lighten the mood but was met with blank stares, "My last name is Karl." He gave in. Sylvia and Liam inhaled. "I know how bad that sounds, but let me explain."

"Karl, As in K. As in Khaos. As in before the Awakening." Sylvia cut in, rushing her words. The more she said, tripping over her own mind. She said them as statements, seemingly simple ideas. "*Before?* Oh, my God. So this means while you were with my sister, while you were engaged, *during* the wedding, you were a part of The House? A military man of the United States of America in The House?"

"Sylvia, I know. I know it's horrible. Just let me explain."

Sylvia moved from her chair and went to stand by the window, she felt dizzy and she reached out to hold the countertop. She wanted it to stop but William wouldn't stop, he stood up too. He continued talking, frantic, "I joined the military young, as you know, and suddenly I was swept into this new program. It was an honor, it was a privilege to be a part of this program. I was moved to a new facility, you remember, don't you? When I was transferred? I wasn't allowed to say anything other than that, it was a complete secret. I was brainwashed, I thought I was serving my country. We learned new rules, and were taught new things. I didn't think it was weird. I mean maybe I had a few suspicions, but I always thought of what a privilege it was to be a part of this special program. I had no idea what I was in, I was happy. I was engaged to your sister! Your sister... I didn't know anything until the day we got married. When the church came down and..." William's voice broke, it looked like he was about to cry.

"I lost consciousness. When I woke up you were there, a complete mess. I was a mess. I mean there was your sister laying there... there was my town in ruins. I, well, I waited. I waited for you to leave the church because at that time my mind wasn't working. All I could think about was your sister. I wasn't in the right mind to take care of you. And I know I'm making excuses now, but I don't mean to. There is no excuse. I'm just trying to explain to you what happened."

Silent tears fell down Sylvia's face and Liam sat in shock on the couch, William continued, desperate for someone to understand. "I went to the only place left. The only place I knew was still standing. My base. That's when I learned about The House, that's when I learned that I had been secretly taken out of the U.S. government and put into The House. But I was overwhelmed with grief. I had already learned the new rules and memorized the lessons. The things they wanted, peace and happiness and protection from the war, those things didn't seem so crazy in the moment. They were things I wanted. And so I didn't fight back. It's not like I could prove The House started the war. No one could, and even if someone could, well, no one could stop it at that point. I wasn't in the right mind to join the resistance, or to do anything but go along with it. I needed a new world, a new environment, I needed to make a new me because the old one involved your sister and your family and I just couldn't think of that any longer. I already had a place in The House, and I just thought I could build off of it. So that's what I did. Time passes and I think about that decision all the time. I don't know if it was the right decision, but I know it's the only one I could make at that time in my life." William paused, Liam had moved to resting his elbows on his knees. Sylvia continued to stare out the window. "Sylvia, I'm so sorry."

Sylvia paused. She didn't know what she had expected to hear, but that wasn't it. "You're sorry? Ha. *You're* sorry? Why? You had no obligation to me. Hell, technically you had no obligation to my sister either, since you weren't married yet! I mean *seriously* William, I just... You were in The House all this time, and I had no idea. And all these years, all these years... just, wow. Just, I, I think you need to go."

"Sylvia-"

"No. *No.* You know what? I've spent years dealing with the loss of my whole family, and my whole life, and my whole reality. I was twelve years old. I was still a kid, *barely* a teenager. I was traumatized, for a really long time. And I could have used someone who was going through the same thing." Sylvia met William's gaze, she had been talking with her hands. She had been racing, and she had even said hell. She never swore. She took a deep breath, checking herself, she gazed down at the floor, "I understand why you did it," She whispered, and Liam recognized the fifteen year old girl who handed out forgiveness like candy, "I just really hate that you did it." She met William's eyes, and Liam saw waves of hurt flood her vision.

William looked down at his hands, "I think I should go."

"Yeah. I think you should." Sylvia finished.

CHAPTER NINE

Chaeronea closed the black door of the office behind her.

Chairman Clementine.

She didn't have enough time to process all her questions, or all the mysteries surrounding the man she was about to meet. Before today, she had had no idea he was here in her community. She still didn't know how long he had been there, or if he had ever left.

His name was idiotic. She knew it, she had always thought it. But there were no rules on names and the power certain ones could hold. No matter how funny his name was, he was always Chairman Clementine, and he was always in charge. He held the most power, he was the ultimate classifier, he was it. He was the main ruler of The House.

And no one questioned it.

At least not out loud.

No one knew about this man, only of the man. He was feared and loved at the same time. Meeting him was an honor and a privilege.

Chaeronea didn't feel privileged.

The first thing she thought as she entered the room was, wow, this place is bright.

The walls of the room were painted bright green and the floor was a light carpeted white. The lights stung her eyes and the temperature was too high.

And there he was, Chairman Clementine, sitting behind his desk.

Damn you Liam. Damn you Liam, damn you. And holy crap it's the Chairman and damn you Liam and you're damn article.

ooo

Liam sat next to Sylvia in the meeting house. Their hands were intertwined and they looked straight ahead. People sat down all around them. They smiled at them and waved and said hello. Other than that, they sat quiet.

"Are you okay?" Liam asked, trying to meet Sylvia's eyes.

"Yes." Sylvia said. She kept looking ahead. She couldn't and wouldn't meet his eyes. Meeting his eyes would break her. According to her, she was fine. She was fine, and she would be fine as long as she didn't meet his eyes.

"You sure you're okay?" He squeezed her hand.

"Yes."

They sat in silence.

Liam sighed, "Sylvia."

"I'm fine Liam, honestly." But Liam grabbed her chin and slowly moved her eyes to meet his. His eyes showed compassion, hers showed a little girl. Her mouth opened, she wanted to say something.

"Hey everyone, is this my seat?" Matilda came rushing in and Sylvia dropped Liam's gaze again.

Liam looked up at Matilda over his left shoulder, "Yeah, this one's for you." He told her, indicating the chair she was standing next to.

Matilda took her seat and leaned over to Liam, "Is Sylvia okay?" She whispered.

"Yeah. Just a long day." He answered while looking at Sylvia.

Click. Click. Click.

Chaeronea walked across the stage to the podium. She shuffled her papers and looked up at the crowd. Everyone fell silent.

"Algo pasó." *Something happened.* Sylvia whispered to Liam, speaking in Spanish; an easy one for her, she was tired.

"¿A la comunidad?" *To the community?* Liam whispered back, eyes forward.

"No. To Chaeronea." Sylvia switched back.

Liam's mind started to get stuffy. Suddenly, today's event with William was swept out of his mind. He started to go back to the article he wrote and the consequences it must have had. He was reminded that Chaeronea had had to deal with that today, and he hadn't been there to claim responsibility.

But he had been there for Sylvia, and *she* was who he was supposed to be there for.

○○○

"Chaeronea! Come right in and take a seat, anywhere you like." Chairman Clementine addressed her. Chaeronea went to sit at the closet chair to her, a silver chair to the left of his desk, "Except there! Thank you." He announced as her fingers touched the seat. Everyone knew Chairman Clementine was a bit sarcastic; they had watched his speeches many times, but now he was using it as a weapon.

Chaeronea went to sit in the other silver chair to the right of the desk. It felt cold and stiff, a weird juxtaposition to the rest of the colorful room around her.

She quickly realized that the room was designed to mess people up. Chairman Clementine had drawings up around the room; blueprints and cartoons that seemed to be drawn by him. He had no windows in his office, and Chaeronea wondered why he wouldn't want to see the world he had created.

Maybe instead, it was to make sure no one saw what was really outside. Chaeronea didn't know exactly where she was, she had been taken through a lot of tunnels to get here, but she knew for certain that Clementine didn't want anyone knowing where this building was located.

Did he have regrets? Would he choose another path if he had the chance? Did he allow himself any of those regrets? When he was a child, was this what he dreamed of? Or had something come along and robbed him of his childhood?

Seconds passed where no one spoke. Chaeronea found her thoughts quickly turning to Sylvia. She had had a few classes with her in school and saw much more of her now outside the school, considering her relationship with Liam. Liam had once told Chaeronea about how good Sylvia was at observing people. He said she could look at someone and tell things about them by the way they carried themselves or their nervous habits. *It's all about determining a baseline,* Sylvia had secretly shared with Chaeronea when she asked about it one night at a dinner party.

Chaeronea was the director of communications for this community. She was in charge of a lot of people and a lot of things. She spent a lot of time organizing and phrasing things to fit the words of The Reining Powers, and more importantly Chairman Clementine. She watched his speeches and read his books. She didn't know what she was doing in that office, but she did know that if anyone could establish Chairman Clementine's baseline, it might as well be her.

Chaeronea didn't attempt to think she could outsmart the Chairman, but she could definitely put up a fight.

ooo

Liam and Sylvia watched as Chaeronea started her speech. "Welcome, Community members, to Friday night meeting. As you all know, we have these meetings every Tuesday and Friday nights, that is: two out of six days of the week. The Reining Powers appreciate your attendance, as members of this community and members of the even bigger House, your attendance helps build an environment of fellowship." She used the same introduction as she did every meeting, but Liam felt something in her voice. A waver or uncertainty, as if she didn't want to be saying it again. As if she was bored of it, or just overall unsatisfied with what was coming out of her mouth.

She continued, "Tonight, Chairman Clementine has a special message he wants me to convey to all of you."

Liam inhaled; Chairman Clementine, a name Liam despised. Liam didn't want to blame the damaged world they lived in on The House, because The House was a community of people who had been brainwashed or forced into acceptance. He also couldn't blame the Reining Powers because some of them were just as brainwashed and innocent as the community members sitting around him. No, Liam blamed Chairman Clementine, for everything. As teenagers they were taught that the Awakening was a mutual affair; some people even blamed it on the United States itself. But Liam was there. He had seen it happen. He had heard the underground radio stations reporting on the years of the war. He blamed Clementine and Clementine alone.

Clementine. What a stupid name, he thought.

"Dear community members," Chaeronea read, actively trying not to grit her teeth, "This is our tenth year as a community, and although we have no classified holidays for these types of events, I think we should all be very, very proud. Especially since every single one of you have helped build this community back up from the ground after the Awakening." Chaeronea took a deep breath and Liam readjusted his hand with Sylvia's.

Chaeronea made eye contact with Liam as she read. Liam didn't know what this was all about but he was ready to decode everything that came from Clementine's message.

ooo

Chairman Clementine had dark skin and dark hair. He sat with his feet on the desk, leaning back in his red chair.

"So nice to meet you Chaeronea, honestly. I haven't heard very much about you, but from what I've heard in the last 24 hours we will have a lot to talk about. Can I get you some water?"

"I'm fine. Thank you." Chaeronea tried not to sound surprised by his very passive aggressive, sarcastic tone.

"Right. That's good, more for me. Alright, so listen Chaeronea, let's stop beating around the bush. Don't you think? You and I both know why I called you here today."

Chaeronea thought it best not to speak, not to break her chances before he got his speech out and his points across. She sat silent and waited. She was going to sit and wait and not break her pose until he was done.

With luck, she'd leave with a warning.

"It's that article. The article about the myth that happened *before* the Awakening. Tell me Chaeronea, do *you* remember anything before the Awakening?"

Chaeronea knew it was a trick question, no one was supposed to remember anything from before The House came around, "No, Chairman."

"Exactly, this Liam Wood, he's a problem. He thinks outside the box, and we don't exactly love people who think outside the box. It's just not in our philosophy. He breaks the rules and twists the reality that we have worked so hard to create here. This community Chareona, all the communities, The House, it is the only thing worth living for. Not the people you share a last name with, not your lover, not any human being. It always will be The House. The collection of people and jobs and items classified perfectly to fit in a *system*."

Chaeronea nodded her head slowly. He continued, "Wood doesn't seem to care about The House. It seems that he has decided The House is not, in fact, everything. According to *him*, there was more before The House. Which is despicable, putrid, and maybe even unforgivable. You know the rules, you know the way of life. He. Does. Too. I'm sick of this conversation already, because I have worked too hard to have ignorant little people poke holes through my system!" Clementine banged his fist on the table, he had taken his feet off the desk somewhere during his speech.

He took a few deep breaths and continued to talk in a calmer, more threatening tone, "Chaeronea, look. This is the first time anything like this has happened since you became Head of Communications and Wood took on editor of the paper. I understand that, I am a reasonable person. But you must know that this *infuriates* me. I live by a life of classification, much like I taught everyone else. According to me, there are good things, things that support the community, and bad things, things that *don't* support the community." He threw her a threatening look and continued his speech, never breaking eye contact. "Honestly, Wood is a problem for me because he's in the gray area. He seems to be an upstanding citizen, but then this happens! I *can not*, can not, have anything in the gray area. Things in the gray area *don't fit*. Does that make sense?"

Chaeronea shook her head yes.

"Speak up!" Clementine ordered.

"Yes sir, perfect sense."

"Alright then. So here is what I need from you; the reason I have called you in today."

○○○

Chaeronea continued her pre-written speech from Clementine. "Community members, at our tenth year, I must remind you that each and every one of you holds a dire position in our community.

Classification is the only way of life, the only way we have ever known, and it has *always* worked perfectly." Chaeronea paused. She sighed, she was basically reading her meeting with Clementine off of a card. That guy was a broken record.

"Nothing ever existed before the system, my system." Chaeronea continued, "You are all humans, so I understand you are flawed in your ways. I understand how you doubt and question and choose not to believe. But I am telling you now, believing in the system is *mandatory.*"

Sylvia felt a pang of sympathy for Chaeronea. She had to be the messenger, she had to convey words that Sylvia knew didn't come from her heart. As much as Chaeronea wanted to convince herself she loved her community, the system, and what she had always been taught, she just didn't. It went down to the core of her bones, just like half of the people sitting in the room. Whether they were trying to convince themselves differently or not, they *didn't* like The House. They *could* remember things before the Awakening and they *wanted* to color outside the lines.

"It is mandatory because each and every one of you were raised to be polite and have manners. I have slaved over this system, put my heart into it, my blood sweat and tears. If you didn't believe in what I created, it would just be plain rude. None of you created the perfect way we live, I did. I went through a lot, and I have to go through a lot on a regular basis. Do you? No. You get to sit back and relax in a perfect world with the perfect system I made for you."

ooo

Chaeronea un-folded and re-folded her hands in her lap. She didn't break eye contact with him, but she wanted to. She didn't lean back when he leaned forward. She didn't flinch when the bells outside rung.

But she wanted to.

She wanted to scream at him and push everything off his desk. She wanted to rip up his important documents and his life's work. She wanted to run out of his office and scream truths that she wasn't supposed to know; things about the history of the land they lived on, truths about the Beginning and the secrets her job allowed her to learn.

She wanted to do all these things, and that was new for her. She had always wanted to follow The House's rules. She was their cheerleader, in a way. So she wondered what had changed, and the answer came to her.

Suddenly, she wasn't being protected anymore. She was being threatened by the one thing she believed in, the one thing she got her strength from.

She wanted to do all the things that raced through her head, but she couldn't. She wouldn't. Because if she did, then she wouldn't have her life. She wouldn't have the status and the intimidation factor. She wouldn't have her house or her very few friend's or her weekly meetings. She wouldn't even have her name, she would be erased, because she would no longer fit.

The Chairman rapped his fingers on the desk. "I'm not going to do anything to Wood. But I want him watched. I want his *every single move* reported straight to me. I can't decide if he is in the good category, or the bad category. And I want to know." The Chairman leaned in more, something Chaeronea didn't think was possible. "And Chaeronea. If I learn that you are withholding information from me, or lying on your reports, or anything like that, let me make myself very clear. You will find yourself moving from one category, to the other."

○○○

Chaeronea gripped the paper in front of her. She hated the feel of the paper. She hated the stares of the crowd. She hated the taste of his words in her mouth.

She felt weak because she was weak.

She could have stood up and challenged anything that was being said, anything that was being done. She could have refuted everything that they were making her say. But she didn't.

She was weak. She felt weak in her knees and her fingers and the back of her head.

She was a spy, an unintentional mole.

She shuffled her feet together and finished off Clementine's speech with the same 12, hopeless words The Chairman himself told her a few hours earlier.

"The world is black and white, and we like it that way."

CHAPTER TEN

After the meeting Liam grabbed Sylvia's hand and pushed through the crowd to get to the stage. Neither of them watched the people stare as they went the opposite direction of everyone else. Liam's focus was above their heads, looking for the black haired girl, while Sylvia kept her eyes firmly on Liam.

When Liam made eye contact with Chaeronea she ended the conversation she was having with an elderly woman and disappeared behind a black door to the left of the stage. Liam and Sylvia both followed her, never letting go of each other's hand.

They found Chaeronea sitting in a wooden chair at a dark wooden desk. Sylvia stayed by the door while Liam went to stand next to Chaeronea.

"Liam, I really don't want to deal with you right now." Chaeronea started.

"Alright. I'll leave you alone. But only after you tell me how things went today." Liam spoke hesitantly but firmly, and Chaeronea felt her heart melt a bit from the concern in his voice. She shook it off and became increasingly aware of Sylvia's body near his.

"Fine. Absolutely fine."

"Wait, really?"

"Yes. You're off the hook. But *don't* let it happen again." Chaeronea raised her head to meet his.

"Wow. That's great news! Almost... almost unbelievable news." Liam's shocked gaze met Sylvia's eye, who motioned her head towards Chaeronea. "You didn't get into any trouble, did you?" He asked.

She considered telling Liam, she really did, but she felt Sylvia's presence and knew about all that was going on with her. She didn't quite care that Sylvia was dealing with a problem, but she knew that if Sylvia was, Liam was too. Chaeronea didn't want to add more on, she wasn't Liam's responsibility.

"No. Everything turned out fine." She moved her gaze slightly to the right of Liam's face.

"Okay then. Well what was all that from Clementine about?"

"Liam." Chaeronea breathed out, "I told you I don't feel like dealing with you right now."

"I know but-"

"Lee, maybe we should just go." Sylvia chimed in, taking a step forward, and for a rare second Chaeronea was grateful for Sylvia. "Thank you,

Chaeronea," She put herself between Liam and Chaeronea, moving Liam towards the door, "and if you ever need anything, don't hesitate to ask." Chaeronea knew it was sincere from the way Sylvia spoke and the way her eyes seemed deep with empathy. Chaeronea raised her head, met Sylvia's eyes and gave a slow nod.

Liam and Sylvia walked back into the empty hall. They started to move towards the entrance, realizing they had to get home to Matilda.

"You're worried about her." Sylvia started, once they had left the building.

"Well, yeah. I am." Liam started, "I'm really sorry, it's just that it's all my fault-"

"Lee, you don't need to apologize. You can be worried about people." Sylvia laughed.

"Yeah but, I don't want you to think-"

"I would never think that."

Liam looked right at Sylvia, taking a deep breath, "I love you." Liam stated, and that was the end of their discussion, because they didn't need to say anything else.

OOO

Sylvia and Matilda sat at a table in the cafeteria. They had blue trays with a serving of pasta and a glass of fruit juice. Matilda was picking at the cheese sauce while Sylvia read Shakespeare under the table, pretending to listen to her best friend.

"They really should have more options." Matilda ranted.

"Mmm." Sylvia responded.

"I mean, it's outrageous!"

"Yeah."

"But seriously, what if some of us don't like cheese?" Matilda baited her.

"According to The House, humans like cheese." Sylvia countered.

"So you were listening!"

"Mmm yeah, totally."

Matilda was the first one to notice Liam. He was average height for his age, with jet black hair and bright eyes. But she didn't see any of that, she just saw him wandering around the cafeteria.

"Hey, that kid looks really lost."

"Maybe he's new." Sylvia said, never looking up from her book.

"That must be it. I think he's coming over here."

Liam saw their table, with only two girls sitting at the end across from each other, and decided it would be worth a shot. Most of the other tables were full and looked a lot more intimidating. From his perspective, one girl was reading, so maybe it would be easier to sit with a distracted person instead of someone who could look him over and judge his every move.

At least, that was his logic when he went to sit down next to Sylvia.

"Who said that seat was open?" Matilda said, calling him out.

"Oh. I- I didn't know, sorry. I'll leave." And Liam started to get up off the bench.

Sylvia looked up from her book, "Matt, don't do that to the poor new kid." She turned her focus to Liam, and almost forgot the english language. She took in his black hair, his striking blue eyes. "This seat is not taken. Go ahead." She choked out. Matilda gave her a look, and Sylvia's eyes darted back to her book.

"Oh. Thank you." Liam replied, and he sat down. He almost started to talk, but decided against it since Sylvia had returned to her book. He felt weird about this new situation. A large part of him wanted to start a conversation with her, she seemed interesting. He watched her tuck her long brown hair behind her ear, focusing on her book. He wanted her to look at him so he could see what color eyes she had.

Sylvia tried to focus on her book. Did it look like she was reading? Maybe her eyes were going too fast or she wasn't turning the page fast enough. She couldn't let on that the boy next to her was a little distracting. A new face in the sea of monotoned emotions.

"What are you reading?" Liam finally asked her, while Matilda kept quiet.

Sylvia looked up from her book, "Romeo and Juliet," she answered.

Liam nodded his head, "How are you liking it?"

Sylvia thought for a second, "My bounty is as boundless as the sea, my love as deep; the more I give to thee-"

"The more I have," Liam cut in.

"For both are infinite." They finished together.

Green, her eyes are green, Liam thought, looking into Sylvia's amazed eyes.

Matilda looked back and forth between them, "Wow, two nerds at one table. My brain." She mocked, holding her head in her hands like she was injured. Sylvia blushed, looking back down at her hands.

"I love it." Liam said through some laughter, "My name's Liam by the way." And he stuck out his hand.

"Sylvia'" Sylvia mumered, holding out her hand.

"Sylvia." Liam repeated, not letting go of her hand.

ooo

Chaeronea sat on the floor in front of her couch with the black rotary phone in front of her. She wore gray socks reaching halfway up her shins with black leggings and a gray sweatshirt. Her hair was askew from the ponytail she half heartedly attempted to put it in. She looked straight ahead.

The clock struck 10 o'clock, waking her from the daze she was in. Thirty seconds later, the phone rang. She took two deep breaths and moved a shaky hand to reach for the receiver.

"Chaeronea." Clementine's merciless voice rang through.

She talked for an hour, answering questions for him. "He's in a relationship; a House official one, with a woman named Sylvia." Chaeronea hated herself more by the second. "She makes a lot of decisions with him. They're inseparable, and they've been that way since school." Her whole body shook with chills, *betrayer*, her mind screamed. "They live together and have a graduate with them. He goes to her with everything." A pause, "Yes, I would say she is a big influence over him."

By the time they got to the last question, Chaeronea was silently crying. When the session was over, The Chairman hung up first, leaving Chaeronea's line dead and ringing. She dropped the receiver back into place, staring straight ahead into the dark room before her, her sobs echoing around her house. For at least an hour afterwards she sat there and let tears stream down her face.

Alcohol didn't exist during the witness times. Humans were defined as creatures that drank water, milk, and fruit juice. But Chaeronea had seen the way her father relaxed after a drink. Right now, she wanted to feel that way. She wanted to be numb. Within the hour, she soon realized she didn't need alcohol for that. She cried herself dry and found that she felt empty and numb already.

But she wanted to forget. She wanted out.

She learned that night that betrayal left a trail, a watermark, a map. She learned it was going to lead right back to her.

And it left behind a bad taste.

CHAPTER ELEVEN

Sylvia woke up early Saturday morning, despite her best intentions. Liam was still asleep and so Sylvia sat in bed quietly.

She didn't feel worried, anxious, or overwhelmed any more. She took deep breaths and realized that sometime between last night and this morning she had come to terms with everything William had told her. She breathed easy and was surprised at how quickly it had come.

She didn't want to wake Liam, so she reached for her sketchbook on the table next to the bed. She was getting to the end of yet another hardcover pure paper book, having filled it with sketches of people and quotes and stories. She looked around at the bedroom walls covered in her pictures, ones that Liam had carefully torn from her sketchbook and nailed up.

She opened up to one of the clean white pages and drew a globe. She added one land mass with a damaged city sprouting from it. What was supposed to be water, she colored pure black.

She loved when her images had meaning. It was important to her that what she showed to the world, or at least Liam and Matilda, had an impact on people. Her sketchings weren't always dark or scary, she drew lots of happy things; but they always had a meaning, a profounding resonance.

She decided to erase some of her lines, adding numbers and dials that went around the world like a clock. She added a chain, and suddenly it was not just the world, but a pocket watch.

She started to write words beneath it in medium black lettering. It read:

In a world like this, we can't risk wasting our seconds on unhelpful emotions. When something happens, we need to feel it, take it in, and then move on. Because right now, we live in a world where those emotions can be used against us. We live in a world that classifies us as happy or not. When we feel things we can't describe, then we don't fit in their world.

Moving on from those bad emotions, well, it makes sure they don't win.

ooo

Matilda was sitting on the couch when Connor came in holding food and drinks. It was

Saturday, everyone's one and only day off. Connor's host family had gone out that day so Matilda had come over.

"Thank you." Matilda said as she accepted the glass of water.

"Of course." Connor nodded, "Look Matt, I have something I want to ask you."

"Sure. Go for it." And Connor took her hands in his and looked down at her. Matilda got the sinking feeling that something serious was about to happen, and she felt her blood rush to her heart.

"Okay well. We've been together for awhile, and now that we've graduated, I was thinking that we should make our relationship official to The House."

Matilda sucked in her breath. Making a relationship official to The House was a big deal. It was basically as serious as a relationship could be, other than having children. But you were only allowed to have children if your relationship was official. It was a privilege to be approved by The House, but also a challenge. It was a huge commitment, because once you were in a relationship, you were classified as being in a relationship. Once you were classified as being in a relationship, you couldn't change it.

Matilda was thrilled Connor had asked her. She loved Connor, but she was also a little scared at making such a huge step. Liam had asked Sylvia at their graduation, right before the ceremony started. He wanted her to know that whatever happened, he would always be there. Whether it was something scary like Karma Day or just a regular happy moment, and Sylvia had accepted right then and there.

Matilda's heart was light but her head felt weighed down with statistics and practicality.

"Oh, Connor. Wow." She finally said.

She watched as his face ghosted over with disappointment, "I shouldn't have asked, forget it-"

"No! No, I don't want to forget it." Matilda comforted him, "I just need time to think it over. It's a big deal."

"Yeah. Take some time, that's fine." Connor nodded his head, relieved she would at least think about it, "And yes, it is a big step. But it's a big step I want to take with you."

ooo

Matilda had returned before lunch, and so the three of them decided to go out to Sylvia's favorite deli for something to eat. It was Syvia and Liam's tradition to go there on Saturday afternoons, so they buttoned their jackets and wrapped scarves around their necks. On their way down the street, Liam hooked arms with Sylvia.

As they turned the corner, Matilda decided to tell them about her big news.

"I was with Connor today." She started.

"Ooh." Sylvia said as Liam kept quiet. He didn't necessarily like to picture Matilda and a boy hanging out together. Alone.

"Yeah. And, well, he asked me something."

"What was that?" Liam asked, but both him and Sylvia already had a feeling of what the answer was.

"He asked to make our relationship official to The House." Matilda confidently shook out. By this point they had stopped walking due to the news, and Sylvia jumped up and down hugging her friend, "That's amazing!" She said. Liam stayed silent.

"Hold on, hold on." Matilda continued, "I haven't agreed yet," she giggled as they continued walking.

"Why not?" Sylvia countered.

"Well, we haven't met him yet, for one." Liam piped in, causing both girls to look at him.

"We don't have to meet him, if it's love it's love!" Sylvia waved her hands around.

"Thanks for the support V, but again, I haven't decided."

"I still think we should meet him." mumbled Liam.

"What's holding you back Matt?" Sylvia asked her.

Matilda started to talk about what a big commitment these things were, how she was afraid of what would happen if they ended the relationship, and how she didn't quite know if she wanted to be tied down to one person.

"Well that's ridiculous," Liam spoke, to everyone's surprise, "Like Sylvia said, if it's love it's love. You just know."

"Aren't you a softie Mr. Wood?" Sylvia said, leaning up against him for effect.

"I'm just saying." He blushed.

"Hey." Sylvia changed topics, "Do you see that man in front of us?" At this point, they were on the same street as the deli and a crowd of people had gathered outfront. Tables were sitting in the middle of what used to be a road; some people sat around the tables, while others waited to make an order at the counter.

Sylvia pointed out a man who stood looking down the road in their direction. He had shocking white hair and black glasses. Sylvia recognized him as the man who had come into her shop looking for peppermint sticks. He wore a black and white plaid collared shirt, a black suit jacket, black leather gloves, and dark blue jeans. He was older, with past years hanging around him; but he had an air of carelessness, as if his years had given him a sense that nothing mattered in the world; that it all passed eventually.

"I know that man," Matilda said, as they continued to walk closer to the deli, "He gave me directions to my job on my first day. Seems like a very nice man."

Liam looked at the girl to his right, "But I told you I would give you directions if you needed them."

"I know but-"

The white haired man started to walk towards them while the two continued. They argued while Sylvia listened until all three of them were aware of the man steps in front of them. Liam was about to introduce himself to this supposed passerby when the man reached into his suit jacket and pulled out a handgun.

Everything happened so fast.

Matilda was screaming when he pointed the gun at them.

The people at the deli, harmless bystanders, stood up to get a look at the scene. Some realized what was happening before others. A woman with a small baby started to cry. Men and women scattered, while others ran forward to help. Except they stopped short because they didn't know how. How do you fight back against a gun?

You can't.

Sylvia fell down with a shot. The bang of the gun reflected off the surrounding walls, causing people to crouch almost simultaneously in fear, and as Sylvia fell Liam's knees collapsed from under him as he tried to reason and think and help the women he loved as blood came from the wound in her stomach. The people around them were trying to escape down the long streets. They thought that Liam would be next, Liam would have thought that too if he was in the right mind set, but instead the white haired man turned slowly around and scanned the running, screaming crowd until he found who he was looking for, and then he shot her, and her, and her, until ten other women laid dead on the cold concrete, motionless.

Matilda's vision blurred even with her glasses on, she couldn't think and the unrealistically loud *pang* of bullets made her cringe and duck every time he fired his evil gun. All she could think was how he got the gun and who he was and why he was doing this in the first place and she kept urging her mind to focus on Sylvia but she couldn't find her, she couldn't reason where she was in relation to the buildings spinning around her and suddenly the bullets stopped and there was a clink of metal against the hard tar ground. People started to notice, and the screaming stopped and the bangs and the pangs stopped but the hurt didn't. It swelled around everyone and seeped through people and dripped down the sidewalk like the dark red of victims blood spilling out.

And suddenly all she could see was blood and red and red and then, darkness.

Liam didn't see Matilda pass out behind him. He had caught Sylvia's head before it hit the ground and he rested it on his lap while his hands held her bleeding stomach but there was so much blood that Liam wondered when it would stop because Sylvia was so small and he didn't think she could possibly have that much blood but it kept coming. Liam's hands were over the spot where the bullet cut through Sylvia and he pressed down because he thought that maybe if he did that like the people in the movies he faintly remembered did then maybe he could save her and maybe he wouldn't lose her.

Because he couldn't lose anyone else, especially not her.

Death is different than kids think it is, different from how they pretend it is. When children play and act out death they fall to the ground, shaking and writhing. They yell out in fake pain and slowly and slowly decrease their shakes until they give one final spazam and lay still. They close their eyes, because they think once your heart stops and the breath comes out of you, you still have the ability to control your eyelids.

But that's not what it's like at all. You don't have any control.

Liam had experienced a few people passing in their sleep, or heard rumors about the people who disappear in the community, but never in his life did he think he would be holding his love as the light started to leave her eyes.

He briefly considered screaming for help, but quickly realized there wasn't anyone to come save them. Sylvia was the closest thing to a doctor they had.

His tears stained his cheeks and he supported her head and rocked her back and forth, crying her name because all he wanted was for her to open her eyes and say something and stand up and be mad and sad with him, but she couldn't do that. She could only open her eyes, and when she did, she smiled.

She reached her hand up to touch Liam's cheek, and her eyes sparkled with ideas and realities and opinions, but no regret. Her eyes didn't reflect any of the anger sparkling in the back of Liam's. They were green swimming pools of bittersweet emotions laced with a content dedication.

Sylvia reached for the hand Liam was using to stabilize her wound and she started to move it away. He protested and shook his head, because he didn't want to move his hand. He wanted to help and this was his way of doing something in a situation where he didn't know what to do. But Sylvia's eyes pleaded with him so he finally moved his hand, his tears falling on her stomach instead and letting Sylvia guide his hand to her heart.

She placed his hand in the center of her chest, and encompassed it with both of her hands. Her heartbeat was unsteady, but Liam could feel the *lub-dub* of it trying to continue its job.

She left her hands there for a minute, until deciding to move them back to her stomach. And while Liam whispered sweet words into her ear about how everything was going to be fine, she was going to be fine, they were going to get through it, he didn't know who he was saying those things for, and she felt his wet tears on the side of her cheek.

And when he whispered *I love you* for the thousandth time, the light left Sylvia's eyes and her body felt different in his arms. Her eyes stayed open, but there wasn't anything filling them anymore. There was no more Sylvia behind them.

And Liam stayed there rocking himself back and forth with Sylvia in his arms. Even when officials came to the scene, and Chaeronea ran up to him and tried to pull him away.

And that was the day Liam Wood swore he truly, completely, absolutely hated the world he lived in.

Part Two

"Let me have war, say I: it exceeds peace as far as day does night; it's spritely, waking, audible, and full of vent. Peace is a very apoplexy, lethargy; mulled, deaf, sleepy, insensible; a getter of more bastard children than war's a destroyer of men."

William Shakespeare, *Coriolanus* IV.V.222-226

CHAPTER ONE

Liam couldn't sleep without her.

Last year, Sylvia had gone away for three days. She had been asked to teach a class to the students early in the morning so they had her stay at the school.

At night, Liam would toss and turn. It was too hot and too cold at the same time. The pillow was too lumpy, but the other pillow was too soft. His legs ached and he needed to stretch and have them crack and go back to the way they usually felt, but nothing worked. All he could think about was the empty side of the bed that Sylvia usually stretched herself across.

So when she got home, he wrapped her in his arms and rested his head on her head. After a minute she pulled back and smiled up at him, wrapped in his arms, "How are you?" She asked him.

"Fine. Better now." He smirked.

"You look like you haven't slept." She told him.

He shrugged, "That's because I haven't."

Now, Liam turns over in his bed to the same empty spot, the permanent one, the one he needs to get used to, or else he will never sleep again.

ooo

Chaeronea is running.

She has to avoid tripping on bodies and slipping on blood or hitting a crying family member.

It's the obstacle course from hell, she thinks.

She sees who she is looking for. He's bent over another body lump, and when Chaeronea sees the long brown hair and signature purple coat, Chaeronea almost throws up.

She's looking around, but the officials are busy with other bodies, and Matilda has passed out behind him. The events are blurry, but she distinctly remembers a few details.

The way Liam's hands weren't his usual skin color, and instead, stained red with blood that wasn't his.

The flash of his black hair as he shook his head *'no'* when Chaeronea tried to pull him away.

The emptiness of Sylvia's eyes.

Chaeronea did everything she could for him. She tried to move his head away so he wouldn't see Slyvia. She tried to move him away, but he wouldn't budge. So she wrapped her arms around his neck, her face over his shoulder so she wouldn't have to look at the body in his arms. She held him there until they yanked Sylvia away, and watched Liam try to put up a fight. She let him cry into her shoulder, and when they had bagged Sylvia and cleaned the street of all the evidence, all the blood, she listened to him whisper, gently, with no anger in his voice, "They will pay."

But in her dream, Liam turned his head to her, looked her right in the eye, and told her, "You will pay."

Chaeronea woke up in a cold sweat. She sat straight up, and took a minute to remember where she was. That day had been haunting her. Sylvia had been haunting her. But mostly, Liam had been haunting her.

For the past week, she had been having the same dream. She couldn't shake it because deep down, she knew she was responsible. She didn't pull the gun out, but she gave Clementine the name.

She killed Sylvia Blue.

Chaeronea doesn't remember getting off the bed and walking to the kitchen. She doesn't even remember picking up the gleaming silver knife from the countertop. What she does remember is the cold tile beneath her body as she sat against the black cabinets. She remembers the heavy weight of Liam's voice in her ear, and her thoughts pounding inside her head.

When the sharp tip of the blade touched her skin, her arms and legs erupted in goosebumps. The hair on the back of her neck stood up, a warning sign, but it was impossible for her to listen to it with the words *betrayal* and *killer* in the back of her mind.

Liam would want revenge. So Chaeronea would save him the trouble and do it for him.

A life for a life.

She dragged the knife across her wrist, but only got half an inch before passing out at the sight of her own dark red blood.

In her subconsciousness, she cursed herself for not being able to go through it.

In her mind, everyone would be better off for it.

○○○

William paced his bedroom, mulling over everything. Here he was in a government issued and decorated apartment, doing a government job, wearing a government uniform, questioning his government.

And all he could think was, *good things they can't read minds.*

Granted, the word 'government' didn't exist. According to the Reining Powers, it never did.

Because of William's position in the community, he knew some secrets others only had speculations about. For example, he knew that the Reining Powers thought 'government' was too controversial to use. He knew that although what was going on was just like a government, maybe even worse than the one before the Awakening, no one was allowed to make the comparison. The Reining Powers also acted like everyone followed that rule; they had fooled themselves into their own imaginary bliss.

William had found out on Saturday night when some of the other patrol men in his apartment building came home from the scene. He had to hide his shock. He had to hide his dizziness, and his pain. He wasn't very good at it, and pawned it off as something he ate, telling the others he needed to lie down. They couldn't know how much he had cared about Sylvia. They couldn't know how much pain he was in when she died.

William paced his bedroom, because if he stopped he would cry, scream, or hit something. Everything she had said to him was right. He had left her when she needed him most. She had been his responsibility. It didn't matter that they weren't blood relatives, or if he never finished marrying her sister. She, Sylvia, was the only one left. The only thing left connected to Before. *Before,* when everything was better, and he was in love, and he was happy and things were normal.

And now she is gone.

And William was left to realize that the Before was gone. Something he never would have imagined. He no longer had something connected to his old life: this new life, new job, new him *was* the reality. He felt the same way he did when he had waited for Sylvia to walk out of the church before him.

William sat down on his bed and rested his elbows on his knees. He put his head down. This whole week he had been emotional. Weird things made him feel sad and lonely and he hadn't spent any time confronting his feelings. His whole body shook because he was finally trying to process what had happened, things that had even happened years ago he had pushed from his mind.

William stood up and lifted his gray mattress off his gray bedspring, finding a beige folder before going to sit back down on his bed.

The folder contained copies of Sylvia's documents, with a picture of her stapled in the corner. When William was given the job of patrolman and assigned to his section, he was given the documents of the community members who lived there. That's when he found Sylvia. Until he had opened that folder, her and her family had been in the back of his mind. He learned her height and weight, her schooling records (which were perfect, he remarked happily), her workplace, relationship status, her lie detector test at the beginning of the Awakening. He had read and re-read the file ten times before taking a single breath. His past had rushed upon him, and he needed to brace himself for seeing her again.

She was nothing extremely special to him, but he reminded him of her, Wallace. The one he loved, who had been taken from him the day they were supposed to get married. He couldn't stop himself from wandering over thoughts of Wallace whenever he was awake, and she haunted his dreams.

Now, as he looked at her picture, and her details, he realized he was holding a forbidden piece of information. According to The House, Sylvia didn't exist, and had never existed. When she died, she had been erased.

William shivered at the thought.

The fact that so suddenly someone could come back into his life, and leave just as quickly. The fact that *before* the Awakening Sylvia didn't exist, and *now* she didn't exist, chilled his bones. The House had enough power to *erase* people, and no one understood the enormity of it unless they experienced it first hand.

William tore out the contents of the document page by page and crumpled them into balls, throwing them in the trash. He was done having the people in his life be controlled by The House. He was completely finished with his past.

According to him, his life started when he joined The House and ended when he died. He didn't want to feel or deal with how messed up everything had become, so he decided to just stop.

In his government issued clothes, in the room the government had given him because of his government job, he decided to be exactly what The House wanted, because that way nothing could be taken from him ever again.

ooo

Wallace and William sat on the brown plush couch, his arm around her, while Sylvia sat on the floor on the opposite side. The TV was open to a news channel, and they watched a reporter's face on the screen.

"And now, an update on the meeting between our President and President Clementine at their international summit. We now go to see President Clementine address the crowd outside the meeting house."

The screen changed to Clementine's face outside a white building, with microphones surrounding him.

Clementine spoke, *"I am infuriated by the way the President of the United States acted towards me today. We make no impossible requests, we just want to be heard and acknowledged as a country with equal weight as any first world country. And as this country we wish to be acknowledged as, we want to start trade and commerce with other countries such as the United States. Is that really so much to ask? After we have fought so hard for our independence?"*

"I can't believe this!" Wallace started, "It's all propaganda! They didn't fight for their independence, they broke into that country and *tore* it from the natives."

"Exactly, and now he wants the country he illegally took to be given status." William added.

"Shh! I'm trying to watch!" Sylvia said, keeping her eyes on the screen.

"I refuse to go back inside and listen to more of these ideas. If the U.S. does not want to recognize us, then we will have to take harsher measures. We have worked too hard for this disrespect."

"Wow." Wallace started again, "Just, wow. I'm glad we have a president that recognizes a psychopath when he sees one."

"That Clementine is trouble. We know all about the violence that went down in his country, but the boys at the base are thinking he might start bringing that violence over here."

"What does that mean for the country?" Sylvie spoke up, and William and Wallace both turned to her, remembering she was listening.

"None of that will happen. The U.S. is too strong." Wallace elbowed William while assuring Sylvia.

Sylvia tilted her head back to the screen as their president got up on stage to address the crowd. He talked about how we should rest easy, because he would not make deals, or work with someone who was capable of so much violence. He would not let that man into our economy, and he was outraged by the way he negotiated.

Sylvia sat there and wondered who the hate had started with. She wondered what a war in her country would look like. And she wondered if the president was making the right decision.

CHAPTER TWO

Matilda knocked on the closed door of Connors house in front of her. She had a heavy green backpack on her shoulder and three scarves wrapped around her head.

Since Sylvia died, rumors had circulated about what happened that day. The most widely accepted one was about how The Teacher from 20 years before had come back, just as promised. They speculated that this time he targeted women in relationships, since everyone he killed fit that category.

Connor had asked Matilda to make their relationship official to The House and she hadn't seen him since. She was too busy caring for Liam and sinking in her own grief. But today she had realized the danger she would be putting Connor in, and herself in, if she accepted his offer. Especially since there was a killer on the loose who was targeting people in a relationship.

Matilda had woken up and packed a bag with her valuables, clothes, and everything else she needed. She would not give up Connor, she would not reject him, but she couldn't stay. She felt guilty for leaving Liam alone, but she couldn't be in that house, the house that reminded her of so many good things. Every moment spent there she felt a pressure building around her, and hours went by where she just wanted to scream into the open space.

She was filled with a grief and a realization in that house. Something that sunk down on her, covering her mouth and nose, so that she couldn't breath, couldn't speak. She constantly wanted to punch something and stretch the stress out of her limbs. She had to do something for herself.

Here she was on Connor's doorstep, ready to pack him a bag. They could be transferred from this community to a different one. Her past didn't have to follow her.

So she stood there and she waited to bring Connor with her to a place she didn't have to explain and a place where she didn't have to feel what she had been feeling the last week. When he opened the door, she kept a smile on her face and tried not to show the pain behind her mask. He took in her face, the face he hadn't seen in days.

"Hey." He started, nervously. What had happened to her?

"Hey." She smiled. What *had* happened to her?

ooo

Liam woke up and stretched out on the bed. His head hurt and his back hurt and his knees hurt. There were no seconds before he remembered what had happened. There was no bliss as he woke up, no time when he just forgot all about it.

He felt bad that he wanted those seconds.

He felt bad about everything, all the time.

He got up to get himself a cup of tea, and saw her favorite mug next to his. He sat down at the countertop, next to the stool she used. He closed his eyes and he saw her.

Liam thought Matilda must have gone to work, until he realized it was Saturday so there was no work. He walked over to her bedroom and opened the curtain to find her stuff missing from shelves and drawers. He turned to find a note on the bed with two words printed on it, "I'm sorry."

He held the small paper in his hand and sat on the bed. He read it over and over, but everytime he did, it was only two words. Two words that didn't help him.

And that's when he lost it.

First, he crumpled the paper in his hand and threw it across the room. It tauntingly flew through the air, falling after seconds, making him angrier.

Then he shoved the dresser over, letting it hit the floor with a whack. He threw books at the walls, letting pages smack the paint and tear free of their binding. He broke his mug on the countertop and watched as the glass flew around the hot water which splashed to the ground.

He tore her room apart in a rage, but then he started to cry, and his destruction didn't seem helpful anymore and it stopped making him feel better. Nothing could make him feel better, so he fell to the bed and let his tears hit the mattress. He raised his forearm and put it over his eyes so he didn't have to see. He couldn't stop shaking, he couldn't stop himself from feeling this way.

Sylvia always did.

Sylvia was his everything.

He had come to depend on her, and he liked it that way. After she died, he didn't feel a hole in his heart, like people had described to him. Instead he just couldn't feel *himself*. He didn't know who he was without her, and he didn't want to know.

He didn't feel empty, he didn't feel him.

And his heart beat faster and faster and he tried to catch his breath and all he wanted was *Sylvia*.

That. And to kill whoever took her from him.

He rolled over to look through the open doorway and saw Sylvia's pictures on the wall. They were charcoal, black and white. She had always loved charcoal; she loved the mess and the way it covered her hands, smudging the ash and making really dark areas on the page. Liam just thought it was too messy to work with, but he loved her artwork and how she liked to draw people or meaningful images with captions.

Liam had an idea, and stood up to go get Sylvia's sketchbooks. She kept a shelf of them under the counter of the shop, and before he sat down he remembered to grab the one by her nightstand.

Sitting on the floor, leaning against the bed, he flipped through them one at a time. Page by page he looked at her shading and her writing, her strokes and her patches of deep black and bright white. There he was, sitting on the couch. There he was again, shrugging on his jacket. Liam saw himself reflected on the pages of her books. He saw Matilda, and he saw jars of spices and fires in the fireplace. He flipped through and saw pictures with Shakespeare quotes and Bible verses. And he started to cry, because everything she did was so meaningful.

And now that she wasn't there, where would all his meaning come from?

He opened a sketchbook from the year when they had moved into the community. He read through her pages and some of her crazy stories, until he got to a picture of a heart. The heart was attached to a stethoscope, a very ancient object in those days. There were semi-circles around the heart, showing that it was beating. And around the stethoscope, she wrote words in thick black lines. HATE. And ANGER. Were two of the most prominent. But GRIEF stood out in the corner. And then he read her caption:

No matter what you're going through, you always have a heartbeat. That heartbeat means something. It means you are alive and functioning. It means that you've been given a life, and you can do anything you want with it. It means that however the world tries to crush you, you are still alive. They can't touch your heartbeat.

Liam read and re-read, and he finally understood what Sylvia had been trying to tell him when she put his hands over her heart. She didn't want him to stop living. She didn't want him to forget he had a life to live. And Liam didn't know if he was sinking in grief or floating in realization. He felt like he could do this, he could do that for Sylvia. He wanted to do it for her, but that would mean she was really gone.

He finally got to the last sketchbook, her most recent. He opened the hard cover to the first black and white page. Liam remembered that Sylvia had to look in every shop in the community to find this sketchbook. The House had ones made for certain jobs, but she wanted one with character, so she bought it from a secret relic shop. She had been so excited, and Liam told her that he would buy her the next one.

The first page of her new book was a self portrait. You could tell she worked hard on it, and that it took a long time. He remembered finding this in her book earlier that year. She didn't show it to him, but Liam looked at her sketchbooks all the time and always found the drawings she didn't like. He loved them all. He thought she looked beautiful, just like in reality. She had smiled at him and blushed, thanking him for the compliment

He kept flipping through, admiring her work. He looked at all the drawings she called political statements. He read her words and relished in how powerful each piece of it was. On the last page, he found the last drawing she ever made. The world turned into a clock, and he read her words. Again he was enlightened by her, and he wondered about the impact she would have had on people if she were still alive.

He felt a loss that it would never happen and that she could never share her brilliance with the world. But then he just felt the overwhelming need to do something about that. She was gone, and he knew it. But his love for her wasn't, and her dreams for her weren't.

Liam remembered the letter he had gotten yesterday and went to the kitchen to find it. It was addressed to him, and read:

Dear Liam Wood,

Our Director of Communications, Chaeronea Bode, has informed us that you have been taken with illness this week. As you are aware, for an illness you are allowed to take up to one week of time off work. This letter is here to inform you that your week has expired as of today. Please take Saturday off, since it is the weekend, but you are required to report to work on Monday morning.

If the illness persists, you need to approach us to extend your illness period.

Sincerely,
The Reigning Powers

Liam had laughed at the letter when he received it Friday night. At that time he didn't plan on going back to work, and he didn't plan on asking the Reigning Powers for more time off. If your illness wasn't better within a week and you went in front of the Powers, you didn't come back. Not that he was sick, he just had no desire to go back to work.

None at all.

But now, he got an idea. He shoved the letter into his coat pocket and dumped out his messenger bag, filling it back up with Sylvia's sketchbooks. He didn't bother with scarves or gloves, he picked up his bag and left.

She was going to be heard.

ooo

Liam walked right up to Chaeroneas door. His eyes had just finished adjusting to the light and his hands had grown numb but he didn't care. He knocked on her door until she opened it, and when she did he pushed right by her before she could speak. He opened his bag but he couldn't find a place to put down the books. Chaeronea's house was a mess, unlike the perfect, square and tired house Liam had seen a few weeks before.

It was messy and dirty and very unlike Chaeronea.

It looked like Liam's house right now.

"Liam I wasn't expecting you-" Chaeronea started. Her hair was messy and down, and she wore jeans, socks, and a long sleeve shirt. She looked different. Not like the usual professional Chaeronea, just normal, and a little frayed around the edges.

He wondered what had happened.

"I know, and I know I haven't been at work. Thank you for covering for me by the way, I know you told them I'm sick. I'm sorry that-" He said, taking steps towards her, taking her in.

"Don't." She started, "Don't be sorry. I'm um, I'm really sorry about what happened." Chaeronea met his eyes.

Liam ran a hand through his hand, "Yeah, aren't we all." He walked around the apartment, "So how are things at the paper?" He tried to ease into a conversation, he didn't want to talk about Sylvia with Chaeronea.

"Busy." Chaeronea said, following along. "The Reigning Powers have had some really strict guidelines on..." She thought about her next words, "recent stories." She finished.

"To cover up what happened." Liam corrected, "It's fine, Chaeronea, I want the truth. Don't worry about me." And he tried to smile. "What happened here?" He asked, montioning around to the scattered mugs and the piles of papers.

"Oh. I just haven't gotten around to cleaning."

"Chaeronea, I know you." He said, looking up at her, "This is more than that." He said as he walked closer.

She shrugged him off, but he grabbed her wrists, slightly below her scar. Thankfully he didn't notice, and she looked into his eyes. "I just haven't been feeling so great since..." And she trailed off again.

"That makes two of us," Liam whispered.

They stayed like that for a minute, because neither one of them were stable, and two negatives make a positive. It just seemed to make sense, them standing there at that moment. The world around them seemed to swirl, continuing to exist without any thought.

But Chaeronea was filled with grief. She felt responsible for Sylvia's death because she had told Clementine all about her. It didn't matter that Liam didn't know, or that Clementine would have figured it out eventually. She knew what she did. And here she was, standing with Liam, his hands around her wrists, and as much as she wanted it, it felt wrong. She couldn't do that to him, or to Sylvia. She felt like a horrible person, and her world reflected that. Not only was her house crumbling, but she was, because she hated herself for what she had done.

She was going to pull away, she wanted to, but he did first.

"I'm, um, well, I'm here because I need your help." He let his hands fall to his side and he shifted nervously, moving towards his bag.

"Oh, okay. With what?"

Liam sat down on the couch and brought the books out. His voice felt choked, "I, I can't let her go like this Chaeronea." He brought his eyes to match hers, "I can't."

Chaeronea went to sit down next to Liam, "I'll help. I'll do whatever you need."

And she wondered if she was doing this to help him, or herself.

CHAPTER THREE

Monday morning Liam woke up early and got dressed. He put on good clothes and nice black shoes. He got to the newspaper before anyone and hung his coat on the first hook. He sat in his office until people started coming in.

Chaeronea was there first. "You're late," Liam smiled.

"Actually, I'm early. And you are too." She smirked back.

"I was earlier," he pointed out, and he watched his employees' faces as they came in and saw Liam sitting at his desk. They seemed happy to see him, which made Liam happy too. Chaeronea stayed in his office with him as he sweated and his heart beat faster with every second and every person who came through the creaky door.

When everyone was in, he called a meeting. He stood in the main office with everyone seated at their desks in front of him while Chaeronea stood in the back.

"Hello everyone," Liam started, his voice shaking. "I know you haven't seen me in awhile, and that's because the love of my life died in the shooting last week."

Silence. He closed his eyes, and he saw Sylvia. He remembered his beliefs and took a deep breath. He felt her standing next to him.

"I know what you're all thinking," he continued, "I was supposed to say I was sick. And I wasn't supposed to mention Sylvia. Because now that's she gone," He paused, the first time he had ever said that out loud, "The House believes she never existed. But I'm not okay with that, I can't live with that, because Sylvia did exist. I loved her, more than anything in the world, more than even myself." Chaeronea moved her gaze to the floor, she wouldn't let him see her cry.

"So, I know I'm breaking rules here, I understand all that. But listen to me, I don't want to live in a world where this is allowed. A world where peoples names can be erased off the face of the earth, their lives crumpled and thrown away like a piece of paper.

"Our world- well, our world is on fire, it's bleeding through its eyes and ears, gasping for breath and closing in on itself. It's suffocating me, and you, and it suffocated Sylvia.

"This is what I believe. This is what Sylvia believed, and this is what you all have thought about at one time or another. And right now, right here, you don't have to deny that. You can believe anything you want in this room, and if you want to constantly switch sides, that's fine too. No one is going to stop you."

Liam took a deep breath, the room seemed to have stopped moving, lifeless, in a peaceful anticipatory way.

"Listen everyone, I'm asking you for a huge favor. I want to start something, right here and right now. I want to start something that The House and the Reigning Powers won't like, and I want your help. I want you to help me change a rule, one rule. The rule that says we can't mourn. The rule that says human life doesn't matter, that it can be erased whenever they want to erase it. If you join me, it means you can't tell anyone, you can't report us, you have to be loyal. But it does mean that you can believe anything you want, for however long you want. When we're done, you all will be the first to get people to listen, and it means that when you die, people will be allowed to remeber you." Liam choked again, "I'm asking you for your help, to share Sylvia's beliefs. I'm asking for help fighting back. Please." Liam looked at each face around the desks.

Someone stood up, "This is ridiculous. This is an act of declassification! I won't report you Liam because you're not in the right mindset right now. But I *will not* join you, and anyone else who does is insane." And he stood up and left, with three others following him, slamming the door behind them.

Liam spoke up, "For those of you who can't risk it, who don't want to stand with me, then you can leave. Nothing will be put against you, and if we go down, you won't come with us. I promise, my name will be the only one in danger, you are all safe whether you leave or not." Two people got up, they whispered apologies, things about how they had significant others to go home to, and Liam understood it. Then he looked around. Five people were left, and they stayed seated, waiting.

Silver started clapping first, not sarcastic clapping, but honest applause. Chaeronea joined in, and met his eyes across the room. Everyone started to join in.

This was what he needed.

Not to get over her, or to forget about her, but he needed it so that he could believe what they both had believed, and to be allowed to talk about her.

Because if he couldn't, he wouldn't be able to do anything again. He was never getting over Sylvia Blue.

ooo

William woke up at 6am and made himself a cup of the strongest tea he could. He had always been a coffee drinker, but The House said coffee didn't exist.

He found the paper outside his door, and sat down to read it.

He started on page one, and spit out all the tea in his mouth, leaving a soaking wet paper in front of him.

ooo

Matilda and Connor sat in the community's waiting room for special services. The two of them had talked all Saturday and packed their bags on Monday. Matilda thought they should be gone by now, but they had been waiting since Monday afternoon, and now it was Tuesday morning.

Connor was still asleep. Matilda had been up most of the night since she found sleeping in the hard plastic waiting room chairs to be unbearable. It was early in the morning and she decided to grab the daily paper and spread it out on the coffee table. She scanned all the pages.

"What have you gotten yourself into Lee," Matilda whispered.

ooo

"Chairman, you're going to want to see this."

"Hand it here," Clementine motioned while taking a bite of his breakfast, studying documents in front of him. He grabbed the paper and glanced over at it, returning to his other documents.

He looked again.

He stared at the headline.

"Ugh," he started, "Tuesdays."

ooo

Liam and Chaeronea sat on the floor in Liam's office with a paper spread out in front of them. It was currently 6:03 AM Tuesday morning and they both knew that three minutes ago replicas of the papers in front of them had been distributed all over the community.

"So." Liam started.

"So." Chaeronea finished. She was there to help Liam, but she had selfish motives. She wanted to right her wrongs, to settle the balance. Because of that, she didn't feel comfortable talking around him. It felt like there was a weight in the middle of her chest, making it hard for her to breathe. But at the same time, it felt like that weight would come bursting out her mouth and ruin everything. She felt like she had to tell him, but she knew the consequences if she did.

He would hate her.

He would hate her because she killed the love of his life.

Accidently.

But her mind skipped over that and straight to blame. He would hate her, and she already hated herself.

But if *he* did, it would be so much worse.

"Hey, are you okay?" Liam poked Chaeronea, jolting her out of her daze.

She couldn't do it.

"Yes. Everything's fine." She said, meeting his eyes. She would show strength, she wouldn't budge, because the weight in her wouldn't budge either.

Liam kept his eyes on her, but eventually moved to look back at the paper.

"We just shook the system." He said in disbelief.

"We did."

"I can't believe I didn't do this sooner."

"You weren't fighting for anyone before now." Chaeronea answered, but before Liam could respond, there was a knock on the door.

Clack clack clack.

Liam shared a look with Chaeronea, eyes wide. Chaeronea's face asked what they should do, and Liam just kept quiet.

But it came again, the sound of the door knocker being banged against the metal stand, *clack clack clack.*

Liam leaned against the wall. The lights were out, the room was cool, he closed his eyes.

"Liam, open up. I know you're in there."

Liam shot forward, eyes open. "I know that voice." he whispered. He stood up, but Chaeronea grabbed his arm trying to keep him down, "I know that voice," he whispered more determined, answering her silent protest.

Liam walked to the door and cracked it open to find William standing outside with the paper in his hands. It looked wet, and Liam glanced around to see if it was raining but didn't see any signs of water falling from the sky. Liam thought that was odd.

"You alone?" Liam asked.

William shook his head yes and Liam stood aside to let him in as quickly as possible. Chaeronea stood up to meet him and gave Liam a questioning look.

"Oh, right. You two don't know each other. Chaeronea this is William, Sylvia's, well, her dead sister's fiance. And William this is Chaeronea-"

"Director of Communications in the community. I know you," William finished, putting his hand out, which Chaeronea shook hesitantly, "from the community meetings. You're in on this too?" He asked, raising the paper he was holding.

"I helped." Chaeronea said shortly. She never trusted new people.

"Liam look, we need to talk." William said, and Liam led him to his office. "I can't let you do this." William started as soon as he sat down.

"You can't?" Liam raised an eyebrow.

"No. This is amazing, but it's illegal." William said obviously, very seriously.

"You don't say." Liam responded, bored. What was he doing here anyway? To weigh in on Liam's life choices? He didn't even know William very well.

"I want to help you," William started, "No. I *need* to help you. This is my chance to right what I did wrong all those years ago. I should have stuck with Sylvia, protected her the best I could. But I was weak and stupid and in shock and I just left. And now, she's not here anymore and I can't make it up to her."

"She never needed you to make it up to her." Liam cut in.

"I know, she was always so forgiving. But I need to do this. For her, you, but also for me. And I'm not trying to be selfish here, I just want to make things right. I want to do the right thing this time."

"Wait. Do what exactly?" Chaeronea prodded. She suddenly felt a connection with this man, she was just like him. They were both there for the same reasons.

"I'm going to take credit," William said, "For this beautiful, beautiful paper. I'm going to take full responsibility, so that when they come for you, they take me instead. It's the least I can do..." he started to choke up, "because this paper, it's all you have left of her. And you don't deserve that. If I had just taken her that day, things might have been different." William nodded sadly.

The three of them stared down at the paper. Where the family friendly headline should have been, ***Community Healer Dies In Massacre With Others*** stretched itself across the top of the paper. Where the main picture should have been, Sylvia's drawing of the pocket clock proudly stood. Her artwork was bravely printed all over the pages. Her portraits, her favorite Shakespeare quotes, her political statements. Her captions were bold on all of the pages.

The paper screamed Sylvia. It screamed declassification. It screamed revenge.

Liam had done the impossible, he had almost cheated death by keeping her alive in this paper. Her artwork lived on, and what she stood came with it.

Now the whole community could see her inspirational words and art. They could see the truth about the world they lived in.

William broke the silence, "So, when the officials come to take you away, because they will be coming." William shot him a glance, "I'm going to take your place. I'm going to say it was all my idea. I'm going to go instead."

Liam shook his head, "We can't let you do that."

"But I want to, I need-"

"No. I can't let you, because it would ruin the plan."

CHAPTER FOUR

"Should we bring Chaeronea in?"

Chairman Clementine was standing with his arms on the table and his head bent down, "No." He said raising his head, eyes gleaming, "Bring in Liam Wood. It's about time we've had a chat."

ooo

Liam sat with his legs crossed under him, meditating in the middle of the floor. Meditating was another thing that wasn't recognized by The House since it was commonly used to reduce stress, and according to the rules there was no stress in The House; everyone was happy all the time.

Liam acted cool and collected, even though he was dying inside.

Yes, he felt some relief after he published all of Sylvia's art in the paper. He felt like he was finally *doing* something. And he knew in a couple minutes he would be feeling that same way. But right now, as he sat there on the floor, everything came flooding back to him. All his feelings that he pushed aside as he worked on the paper were exposed as he sat on the floor.

ooo

A pencil came flying at her from across the room.

"Wha-" Sylvia started, already knowing the answer.

He pretended he didn't see her glaring at him with questioning eyes. He kept his eyes on the book in front of him.

But he couldn't resist looking.

She was trying not to laugh, she wanted to be mad. He was trying not to laugh, he didn't want to give himself away.

She stood up and picked up the pencil. Walking over to his chair she dropped it in front of him, giving him a knowing look. She went to sit back down, and sooner or later,

A pencil landed at her feet.

"Would you cut it out?" Sylvia shot back.

"Cut what out?" Liam hollered back, not caring about the other people around them. She could only roll her eyes in response. He could only smile at her.

ooo

They sat next to each other in class. She wiggled her rings off her fingers, fidgeting, setting them down on the brown wooden table in front of her. He picked them up, and put them on. She rolled her eyes at him and he smiled his lopsided grin back.

She really wanted to say something to the teacher, she wanted to disagree with him because he was blatantly wrong. But disagreement wasn't allowed, she knew that, so she tried to keep quiet through the class. Eventually Sylvia couldn't take it. Something she had learned her whole life was just disintegrated by this teacher in five minutes.

Liam could read her mind. He knew, he had listened to her rant about this class in particular.

So she raised her hand, the sweet face of an innocent question.

"Sylvia?" The teacher called on her.

Liam moved his hand to her knee under the table. She hesitated.

"Oh. Nevermind, I forgot." She muttered, lowering her hand.

He had just saved her.

○○○

"Drink this," Liam said, handing her a glass bottle of water.

"I'm fine," She told him, exaggerating the words, "I don't need that." Sylvia stated, curled in a ball on the couch, "Come sit."

She had a raging headache, and before the Awakening they would have called it a migraine. But medical conditions didn't exist now. Even if they did, she wouldn't have admitted her headache to him. She was determined not to show weakness.

According to her, she was fine.

"Come on Sylvia, please," he tried again.

"Come on Liam, I'm fine." She mocked him.

"Oh yeah?" he started with an idea, "Prove it." Sylvia raised an eyebrow, "Stand up."

Sylvia melted more into the couch, she knew she had been defeated. She weighed her options, maybe she could just not stand? Then he would win, and he knew it. No, she had to get up. *Maybe it will be fine*, she thought.

But as soon as Sylvia lifted herself off the couch her head got foggy and the room started to spin around her. She thought she might be falling, but then Liam was under her and suddenly she was sitting on his lap back on the couch.

Liam handed her the water and curled around her. "Hey, don't feel bad, the same thing happens to me." And Sylvia drank the water and wondered if maybe, despite The House, life wasn't so bad.

○○○

Liam's memories were interrupted by keys jingling outside the door.

You might expect them to bust through the door, tearing it off its hinges and storming the room, but The House didn't work like that. They wanted stealth. No one saw them, no one heard them; The House left their people in ignorance.

He was fine.

He wasn't afraid.

He was ready.

Yeah right, he heard Sylvia's kind voice in his head.

So when The House officials, dressed in normal dark clothes, walked through the door, he put on his best smirk. His, *Yep, I'm right here,* smirk. His, *I know why you're here,* smirk.

His, *You can't touch me,* look.

No matter how fake it was.

Liam was walked down the street before one of the men unlocked the door to an old subway station and walked Liam inside. After that moment, it was all black.

He walked for a really long time, tripping occasionally on the rail beneath him or some old rubbish. His hands were tied behind him and some man was pushing him along while simultaneously keeping him from falling flat on his face. Liam felt no need to appreciate him.

He heard the low whistle of someone behind him as they walked, a song The House teaches kids from a young age.

He must be a Khaos person.

And as he thought that, he smiled because he realized that Sylvia and her observation skills had rubbed off on him.

But he couldn't go there. No, he wouldn't.

So his thoughts wandered to Matilda as he walked. She had left so quickly, and Liam had been so wrapped up with everything going on that he hadn't stopped for one second to think about how she must be feeling. Afterall, they had both lost a best friend. He should have been there for her.

Liam tripped and heard the men laughing at him, he rolled his eyes behind the cloth.

He thought of William, realizing that now, they had a lot in common. He was in a similar situation he had been in. Liam wasn't there for Matilda, just like Wiliam hadn't been there for Sylvia.

But Liam was fighting back, so didn't that balance the scale?

He wanted to dislike William and he didn't know why. He felt like William couldn't be trusted, like he wasn't brave enough to go through with their plan, but Chaeronea had taken him aside.

Look, she had said, *I know you don't trust this guy, and I'm having some trouble myself with this, but we have to remember he works for The House.*

So do you, Liam pointed out.

Liam that's not the point, she rolled her eyes, *You have to go through a lot to get a position like his. We may not trust him, but* The House *does. His position doesn't have a lot of consequences like mine. I was put in this job because they knew I was afraid, and could easily-*

Chaeronea don't say that.

No. It's the truth. I'm easily manipulated by fear. But these guys, the patrol men, their position isn't based on fear, because Clementine knows they could cause an uprising. They get the position because they're close to the system. These people have been in The House for a long time *and they are the only people The House trusts with seeing the things they see.*

So?

You are so frustrating! So, he can help us, *Liam. He's more on the inside than either of us.*

Couldn't that be problematic? He could turn on us.

Trust me, And Chaeronea gave him the most honest, serious look Liam had ever seen from her, *That man is trying to balance some deep moral scale. He's trying to right a wrong,* she paused, choosing her words carefully, not breaking eye contact, *and he won't do anything to screw that up.*

So as Liam walked, he thought about the moral scale Chaeronea was talking about. He wondered if someone was really looking down at you counting your wrongs and rights. He wondered if there was ever any consequence for doing something wrong. But mostly, Liam wondered if doing something for yourself, to balance your own scale, meant the same as doing it just to do it.

Liam was pushed forward and up some stairs. He felt each step as carefully and quickly as he could to avoid tripping. Lights flickered and suddenly there were more steps, but he could feel that they were out of the station.

He mindlessly turned corners until he was pushed through a door.

And there in front of him was Chairman Clementine.

Act surprised, he thought.

CHAPTER FIVE

Ryan sat at a black table in a dark room lit by one lightbulb hanging above him. There were wires connected to his fingers which were connected to a machine that ticked along, drawing lines on a paper.

He glared at the man across from him, a small wiry man who held a clipboard, checking things off as he went.

"So, let's start with the basics," the man started, not bothering to introduce himself, "Name?"

Ryan rolled his eyes, "Ryan Smith." He tapped his other hand against his thigh.

The man looked at the machine, nodded his head, and checked off a box, deciding that Ryan was in fact not lying about his name.

"Where were you born?" And Ryan proceeded to answer a bunch of baseline questions about his life, each time having the little man nod his head and check a box.

Ryan tapped his fingers.

"Do you have a wife?"

"No."

"Girlfriend?"

"Nope."

"Any kids?"

"Not sure." Ryan answered honestly, raising an eyebrow. The machine spiked.

"Explain that a little more." The man met his eyes.

"Well, seeing there isn't any judgement here," Ryan said, realizing that he honestly didn't care what would happen, "This girl I was seeing told me she was pregnant. But I don't know how it went, I left before anything could happen."

The machine was stable, he wasn't lying about that either.

Ryan was going through the mandatory lie detector tests every new citizen took. Currently, the world was at the end of year one of the Awakening War, and The House officials had raided a secret underground village of people that Ryan was staying with. Now, he was sitting in a cold metal chair, his jet black hair falling in front of his eyes, answering every question they could possibly ask him. They needed to ask the questions because they needed to classify him perfectly. His favorite things, his background (Which was strictly for their knowledge. His past was to be forgotten by everyone, starting the day he got caught), the things he was good at and the things he was bad at. They needed to put him in a category.

They couldn't *not* know, because to them knowing was everything that mattered.

So Ryan sat down to be placed in a category, or multiple categories, he didn't know. But as long as the little man kept checking boxes, Ryan would sit in that seat.

He tapped his fingers on his thigh.

"Have you ever committed a crime?"

"Yes." Ryan said. He had no reason to hide himself, with the world falling apart around him. He could hide, but then the machine would pick up on it, and he might end up in even more of a mess. So why did he care? If they were going to hurt him, oh well, what did he have to live for? At the end of the day, what was done was done. He believed in his mission, and he was going to stick with it whether this little man or anyone else punished him for it.

People thought what he did was wrong, he just thought it was common sense.

"Honest." the man mumbled at his statement, checking a box, "What did you do?"

Ryan sighed, bored, but turned his mouth into a devilish grin, meeting the man's eyes, "I massacred about five hundred women, scientists, doctors, and government officials in three consecutive shootings."

The man brought his eyes up to meet Ryan's.

The machine stayed straight.

He wasn't lying.

If he couldn't beat them, he sure could scare them.

ooo

Ryan sat there for half an hour before a different man came into the room. He recognized him from the news; in front of him The Chairman sat, the one who had started the wars, and the pain, and the killing.

Ryan respected this man.

They sat staring at each other for a while until the Chairman finally spoke, "You're The Teacher."

Ryan scoffed, "That's what they call me." He thought it was ridiculous, people following his beliefs like a religion.

"Wow," Chairman Clementine leaned back in his seat, "It's amazing to finally meet you! I mean, I *worshipped* you when everything was going on with my country. I didn't quite agree with the way you left things, the whole twenty years note, but hey, we all have our quirks. What I did admire though, was your belief, and how strongly you stuck with it. All these people screaming and crying and telling you you're wrong, and you don't even hear them. It goes in one ear and out the other!"

Ryan blew the lock of jet black hair out of his eyes.

"Some say you're just a little kid, you know that? I understand it, I mean how old were you when it happened? 25?"

"23." Ryan responded absentmindedly.

"Wow," Chairman Clementine said, "wow." He repeated. Clementine was amazed at this young adult sitting before him, but honestly he was also pretty scared. This kid in front of him had *killed* people. Clementine had killed before, but never directly, he always sent people to do it. He had other people press the buttons, or he ordered a matilia to finish off his battle, but never had he taken a gun and actually killed someone right in front of him.

Ryan could tell, and he doubted whether Clementine wanted to be on the same level as him.

So there they sat, an old man running a community he had built after threats, a system that to him, would be perfect. A man who thrived off categorization and organization. A man who had made the decision to end the world most people knew to be normal.

And a cocky twenty year old who prosecuted others based on their decisions.

Clementine thought they were going to get along.

Ryan thought he could use this to his advantage.

"I think we can help each other here," Clementine spoke. And they both smiled.

ooo

Liam sat across the table from Clementine, "I think we can help each other here." he spoke. Using the same words he had used so long ago on another black haired boy.

Liam laughed, "Yeah, right." He needed to stall, buy time. Clementine was visibly frustrated with Liam and he could use that to his advantage. .

Liam counted the seconds of silence. 30, 31, 32, 33. Was he trying to intimidate him? Liam honestly didn't care, he was here for one reason.

ooo

When Ryan was 22 his girlfriend told him she was pregnant.

It hit him like a ton of bricks.

He didn't want to keep the baby. He was young, a fresh new pre-law student at an esteemed school. She was also in school, and they both had dreams and plans. He didn't want to give all that up. But she wanted him to. She had a vision of him and her together with a family, settled down in a big house with kids running around.

She had made that decision. She decided to keep the baby and she wanted him to be the father.

And he hated it. Honestly, Ryan was not ready for that. He didn't like kids. He didn't want kids. He didn't like his own father and he certainly didn't want to be a father.

Ryan went crazy. At least, that's what happened from his parents' eyes, his girlfriend's eyes, his teachers and his neighbors eyes. No one understood what went on in his head. Later, they realized they had missed the warning signs, and the small switches in his personality. They couldn't count the number of days, minutes, or seconds the change in him had happened; it seemed to happen instantly. After the initial shock, they tried remembering him before the change, but they never could picture him right. They could never bring up a full image of him without hints of the sour memories.

When it first happens, there is a lot of blame, a lot of guilt.

Ryan disappeared.

Maybe it was something I said, they think, *maybe I wasn't sensitive. Maybe I should have approached the topic differently. What did I possibly do to upset him?*

You rack your brain, what did you do?

And his girlfriend is the one who hurts the most. No one sees her cry, but they see the degradation in her happiness and they try to get to the bottom of what's bothering her. But she can't tell them, not without him.

And they all tell her to move on.

There is a shooting in Texas.

Of course there are some people who deny it, straight up. His mother, for instance, won't let herself believe anything. The pregnancy, her one and only son running away. Why hadn't he come to talk to her?

The rest of the world was stunned, confused, looking for the culprit. But his family knew, his girl knew, and his town suspected because the newspaper spelled out his description. His hair and his age, and the time fit perfectly.

There were two more shootings.

They read about them in the newspaper, and saw the reports on the TV. They didn't talk about it, how could they? But they wondered why.

And they panicked. Panicked and grieved. This little kid they had raised and loved all his life, the teenager she had fallen in love with, he was gone. They didn't recognize him.

Over and over and over again they asked themselves how it had happened.

He called once, called her.

He was blunt, so very blunt and mean. She didn't feel anything in his voice coming through the gray corded phone she clutched in her hand.

"It's nice to hear your voice." She cringed, why did she have to be so kind to him, after everything he had put her through? But she also couldn't bring herself to be mean to him. She didn't know why, she hated it.

"You're just saying that." She took a deep breath. She wouldn't let him suck her dry. He kept going, "I don't know why I called." he admitted.

"Well, what have you been up to?" She sighed.

"I think you know," he chuckled.

She felt dizzy, "Yeah."

There was silence on both ends.

"Why'd you do it?" She blurted out.

She heard him inhale for a long time, "People need to learn."

She started to cry, she couldn't recognize the frightening voice talking to her through the phone. "Learn what Ryan?" She begged.

"That people's decisions affect others. That it's *wrong* to put someone in a situation constructed by unanimous, pompeus, unthought out decisions. It ruins them."

She felt like a knife was going through her. She tried to convince herself she was being too dramatic, but the truth pounded in her ears. She felt the weight of all those peoples deaths on her shoulders, all because she had wanted a family. All because she loved him enough to want a family with him.

It was so unfair, she screamed to herself, that she had to be blamed for something so horrible. So unthinkable. That she had to live with a voice in the back of her head whispering how awful she was. How dramatic. How condescending. How evil.

Because that's how he made her feel.

And why? Only because she had reacted the way anyone else would react to her new news. She knew what she wanted. She knew what were options and what weren't, and yes, she tried to steer him into some, but he wouldn't take it.

Now he was this, and she was here. And everything was falling out of her grasp. She was crying, and shaking, and she couldn't take anything anymore.

She hung up on him.

At least she would have that.

ooo

Chaeronea's heels pounded against the concrete sidewalk, then stairs, then the wooden floor as she walked into the community's main office building right past the receptionist.

"Excuse me!" the lady started, running behind her to catch up to Chaeronea. "You can't just walk in here!"

"My name's Chaeronea Bode, I'm head of communications of this community and I have a meeting with The Chairman. Now I suggest you get out of my way." Chaeronea told the receptionist, holding out her ID card.

"But Chairman Clementine-"

"Is expecting me, yes. At this pace, I'm going to be late. Now would you like me to tell the Chairman that *you're* the reason I was late?" Chaeronea stopped walking, fixing her eyes on the tall thin receptionist who was shaking her head in fear. "That's what I thought. Don't let anyone know I'm here, Chairman's orders." And she mounted the stairs, turning her back on the woman, smiling. The fear The Chairman instilled in other's could be used to her advantage.

ooo

Over the years Ryan's hair turned white and his eyes quickly started to fail him, so he got black rimmed glasses. He spent his time in The House as an important figure no one recognized. He was their biggest secret, their biggest weapon. He didn't have a four letter last name, because he was too important for one. He was categorized differently than everyone else. Only the people Clementine wanted to know about him knew about him.

He hid in plain sight.

Ryan's main job was to relax and not hurt anyone without a direct order. Although he was close with The Chairman, he knew Clementine had people watching him. Their relationship came with a lot of ultimatums. Ryan was far too dangerous to control; Clementine needed him to move when Clementine wanted him to move, and be still when he wanted him to be still.

For a long time, he had no way to lock that down. Ryan worked in a high sector of The House's army during the Awakening that kept him satisfied. When the war was over, a year later, Clementine kept Ryan as a bodyguard. A hitman. An asset. But Ryan was becoming restless. He had to sleep in a cell, he was constantly watched. According to Clementine he was lucky to be alive, to have a place, but Ryan started to become bitter.

One morning, he was hanging around upstairs watching the kids in school when he recognized one. He recognized the eyes, and the nose, and the hair.

He looked just like Ryan.

And that's when he realized he was looking at his son.

Of course he checked his file. Poured over it, checking every detail.

The birth date lined up.

The last name lined up.

Town.

Age.

Everything.

He stared at the picture of his son in the file and felt a feeling he had felt only in his youth when he would stare at a happy couple in school. He would sit and watch them hold hands and whisper to each other. He remembered turning away at those moments, because they made him want what those people had, and he wanted it urgently. If he could be anyone at that moment, he would be that boy holding that girl in his arms.

He didn't regret any of the choices he made. He didn't want to change diapers, or wake up at 3am, or buy baby clothes. But this boy didn't need any of that now. No, he didn't feel regret, but instead a deep longing. And as much as he didn't want to admit it, that feeling was jealousy. Just like when he watched the couples at school, he wanted that, now. Without the drama and the problems, he wanted it instantly. Just looking at this boy he wished to be a part of his life in any way he could. But with the circumstances they were under, well, there were no mothers or fathers now. But did he want that? Maybe. But mostly he just wanted a connection. A feeling that he was at least a tiny part of this human's life. So he did the only thing he could, he added another ultimatum to his relationship with Clementine.

"*Excuse* me, you want me to do what now?" The Chairman scoffed.

"Immunity. I want immunity for my boy." Ryan didn't hesitate to tell him.

"The kid you abandoned before his birth? The kid you started a religion because of? A kid-"

"It's *not* a religion."

"Well, you better tell your followers that my friend."

"I thought you didn't classify that."

"I- well." Clementine looked up. He knew his own philosophy but honestly it wasn't very air tight. Lots of people poked holes in it, made him run in circles and look like a fool, but Clementine had one thing they didn't: power. They could think however they wanted but they would never tell them his flaws to his face. Fear was his weapon. The problem here was that Ryan wasn't afraid.

Clementine countined, "I'll give the boy immunity. But you have to be completely loyal to me from now on. My beliefs are now your beliefs. You don't talk without permission. You don't move without permission. You don't breathe unless I say so. No more of this, 'I'm the tough guy act.' No more, 'I don't answer to anyone.' I've let it slide because I respect you. But getting all soft for this kid? No. You want immunity, you sell your soul to me."

And Ryan did, and he couldn't explain why.

○○○

"What you've done, it's grounds for declassification." Chairman Clementine spoke. Liam was silent, the Chairman wasn't expecting that. "But I'm sure you and I can come to an agreement, and there won't be any need for that. What do you think?" Clementine challenged.

Why was he doing that? Why wasn't he just declassifying him? Why was Liam even having this conversation? He should be dead.

Not that he had any inclination to be dead, he was there stalling for time and Clementine was making it easy for him. Liam just wanted to know why.

Be smart. Liam heard Chaeronea's voice in the back of his head. *Act grateful, something's going on. Use your cards wisely.*

Liam heard Sylvia's voice too, *Clementine is a terrorist, but he's predictable. Listen in between his words.*

And Liam realized that Sylvia and Chaeronea had more in common than they thought.

"Can I have some water?" Liam coughed, "It's stuffy in here." He faked.

Clementine eyed him suspiciously for a moment before motioning to the only other man standing in the room, the man who had brought Liam in.

"Really?" The man questioned in disbelief.

But Clementine didn't even have to answer, just fix him with a stare that told him there was no room for debate. *It's just water,* Clementine thought. *No harm done.*

So the man left and it was just Liam and Clementine.

ooo

Ryan watched his son grow. He watched the people he grew up with, he watched which classes he did well in and which ones he didn't. He watched his sons dark black hair grow and shorten over the years. But he never introduced himself.

In The House, you were born and then transferred to The House's care. You didn't have a mother or a father, you were just part of The House.

So that was Ryan's excuse. He told himself that the reason he never introduced himself to his son was because it wouldn't have mattered. It's not like he could take his son out to dinner or a baseball game, trying to repair a relationship. The fact that he didn't want to, well, that didn't help him sleep at night. The fact that The House wouldn't allow it, that's what let him get his rest.

○○○

Chaeronea showed her ID card to the guard outside of the file room, and once she got in she locked the door behind her and hoped he didn't notice. She turned around and put her back flat against the door. She was looking for a specific file, but had no idea where to find it.

The great thing about The House's file room was that it was extremely organized. Everything was classified multiple times. One room was alphabetically by last name, the next broke everything into categories of age, and the last room separated between male and female.

So that narrowed it down a bit.

What did she know? She knew he was a man, so she went to the last room, left side, with file cabinets as tall as her. Now, age. Chaeronea did the number in her head. The news said he was 23 when it first happened, now it was 20 years later. So he must be 43. Chaeronea thought that seemed old.

She opened the file box that held 43 year old men. She didn't know his name, just what he looked like. Chaeroneas head raced. She couldn't open every single file until she found his picture, she didn't have the time, so she started by scanning the names. Her heart raced as she looked for something unfamiliar, something special. Everything was normal, four letter last names. Until she saw something different.

Ryan Smith.

She pulled the file out immediately. It was different, this Ryan had a special last name; one that wasn't four letters. So she opened it, and there, looking back at her, was someone Liam had described in great detail.

White hair, black glasses, tall with dark eyes.

The man who had killed Sylvia.

She grabbed his file, and then for extra measure quickly found hers, Liam's, and Williams. It couldn't hurt them that The House wouldn't know every detail of their life. It was a contradiction. Without the file, they didn't exist.

But they were going to cause enough chaos to make The House admit that they did.

ooo

William marched right past the secretary and her questions. He and his fellow patrolmen had ID badges, they weren't technically doing anything wrong.

Yet.

So they walked up the stairs and turned some corners, and then they stood and waited for a man to exit the large wooden door down the hall. Honestly, William laughed at the lack of security this building had. He knew that secruity people were coming, it was a protocol he knew by heart, but they wouldn't get here in time. When the man left, he knew the plan had worked, and he took the cue to walk to the room.

William opened the dark wooden door with his right hand and motioned for everyone to file in. He and his patrolmen stood around the table where Liam and Clementine sat, and Liam stood up to join them. The look on Clementine's face was priceless when he realized his own men were surrounding him.

"What is going on here-" Clementine started.

"I think," Liam cut him off, "this is called a revolt, mutiny, or a break out. Whatever words you want to use, use them. I honestly don't care. Call it what you want, you won't be telling many people anyway." Liam shrugged, "Here's what's going to happen. I'm going to walk out of here just fine, with nothing wrong, or you'll have to deal with these guys." And he motioned to the men standing around him. "Once we're out, well, the next move is up to you. We will give you half a day to publicly admit and mourn the death of Sylvia Blue, and any other women who died in that tragic accident, as well as bring their killer to justice." Liam paused, "Their lives meant something, and that deserves to be acknowledged. We, the people of this community, put up with a lot of stuff. We have *no* rights or any say in what goes on here." Clementine's face grew redder, and everyone was surprised that he hadn't jumped in yet. "So you will do all of this, and you will declare that from this day on people will be publicly mourned and remembered, because they deserve that respect. And afterwards, you can do whatever you want with me; Declassify me because you don't want to admit I'm the one behind your new discovery, or put me on a pedestal because I'm the voice of the new age. I don't care. I honestly don't, as long as these lives are honored. So, you have twelve hours, which is when Tuesday night meetings start. We can't wait to see what happens after that."

Liam turned to leave, satisfied with the shocked expression Clementine wore, but as he placed his hand on the doorknob the Chairman spoke, "What happens if I don't?"

Liam turned to face Clementine again, "Well, then we take it into our own hands, with information I don't think you want in the open." Liam threatened.

Clementine seethed, "I don't negotiate with terrorists."

Liam paused. "I think you're forgetting who the terrorist is here."

And he walked out.

CHAPTER SIX

Chaeronea and Liam sat on the floor of Chaeronea's dark apartment, the shades drawn and the lights off. Liam had taken anything of importance from his apartment and moved it here, because they were certain Clementine had people searching for him as they sat there. It was hard for him to leave that apartment, but he knew it was for the best. The House didn't know Chaeronea was involved, at least not yet, so together they sat on the floor, files in front of them, staring down the clock on the wall. Silence.

"I'm glad it went well," Chaeronea started, "I was worried about what Clementine was going to do when William walked in."

"He may be crazy, but I think he knows when he's been beat, at least for a little bit." Liam said, running his hand through his hair. "I was mostly worried about you." He said easily.

"Oh, well. I was fine." Chaeronea said, not knowing how to respond.

"Right, of course." Liam put out there.

Silence.

"But thank you." She offered.

"Of course." He nodded.

More silence.

"Should we open them?" She nodded to the files. Her file was on top, with Liam's next, then William's, and Ryan's below.

"No, I think we should wait to see what happens. He still has ten hours." Liam said, trying to convince himself. His hands were itching to do something, he wanted to open the files, but he knew he couldn't. He had to keep his word to Clementine, because if he didn't, he wouldn't be any better than him. So Liam stood up and paced up and down the dark room. Chaeronea watched him, but she didn't know how to comfort him like Sylvia had. Eventually, she went to get a glass of water and Liam spread himself out on the gray couch.

"What calms you down when you're nervous?" Liam asked quietly.

"Who says I get nervous?" Chaeronea smirked, handing the glass to Liam and sitting on the ground.

"Well, I thought that since you talk in front of so many people that maybe you get nervous sometimes..." Liam backed down.

"No, no." Chaeronea rushed in, "I was being sarcastic. Of course I get nervous." She said softly, "I take deep breaths, and I've learned to look at certain people in the crowd that make me feel safer"

"Like who?" Liam asked gently, lowering his voice like Chaeronea had.

Chaeronea took a minute to respond, deciding what words to use. As she mulled over what his response to her answer would be she was filled with an anxiety that moved her to her feet, taking her to the kitchen to wash Liam's cup. When she got back, she stood behind the couch he was lying on, took a deep breath, and answered truthfully, "You."

But Liam had fallen asleep on the couch, and Chaeronea thought it was probably best he hadn't heard her.

ooo

"Hey, wake up, Clementine has five minutes left." Liam rolled over to see Chaeronea leaning over him shaking him awake. His vision sharpened to find William shrugging on his coat behind her.

"I fell asleep?" Liam asked in shock..

"Yeah, but we didn't wake you because you haven't really gotten a lot lately." Chaeronea shrugged. It was true, ever since Sylvia died he hadn't been sleeping. He almost felt guilty that he had drifted off peacefully on Chaeroneas couch.

"Cmon, we need to get to the town hall." William told them both.

Liam got up and they all started down the street. They arrived faster than Liam thought they would, and when they got to the town hall everyone was already seated, the conversations that usually filled the time before the meeting were not there. Liam felt strange. When they walked in, they stood in the back of the meeting hall, which Liam also thought was strange. He thought they would want to try and blend in more, to not be seen, but William and Chaeronea were acting like everything was normal, so he did too.

Suddenly, Clementine himself was up on the stage calling the meeting to order. No one in the crowd knew what was happening, to them it was a normal Tuesday night meeting. Clementine started to talk, a whole speech about how he mourns the deaths of the people who passed in the awful shooting, how he had brought the killer to justice, and people were smiling and standing up to clap and cheer. Clementine gave him a smile and a wink, and Liam was so confused because he didn't think Clementine would actually do it. Suddenly Chaeronea was hugging him, but when she pulled away, she was Sylvia.

"Sylvia? What are you doing here? You're dead." He asked her, shocked.

"I am?" She replied smiling, tucking hair behind her ear, "I wanted to say how proud I am of you, for changing things around here. It was stupid and rash..." She smirked at him, "But it worked, and I'm so proud. Honestly, I am." She smiled at him.

"Sylvia- I, thank you. But I don't understand, how are you here, what's going on-"

"I want to say I'm proud, Lee. And look, if you like Chaeronea I get it. Be with her, I'm gone."

"What- who said I want to be with Chaeronea? V."

He tried to reach out to her, but then he woke up.

○○○

William knocked on Chaeronea's door and waited until she let him in. He looked around the dark room as his eyes adjusted, spotting Liam on the couch.

"Is he asleep?" William asked hesitantly, afraid to know the answer. He didn't know Chaeronea very well, and now he was in her house basically all alone. Without Liam there, what were they supposed to talk about?

"Yeah. He fell asleep a couple minutes ago and I didn't want to wake him, he hasn't been sleeping very well." She told him as she went and sat on the living room floor. .

"I don't blame him." William sat across from her. He wasn't used to sitting on floors, and he had to admit that he was at least twenty years older than Chaeronea, which made everything even more uncomfortable. They sat in silence for a bit, neither knowing what to say. Questions banged in Chaeronea head until she finally had to just come out and ask.

"So, you knew Sylvia." Chaeronea started, a statement hanging in the air.

"Yes. I was going to marry her sister." He replied, and the room's warm air swam around his words. No one knew where they were heading, but at least a conversation had started. Both Chaeronea and William felt a huge weight lift off them.

"Right. I think Liam mentioned that." She added, looking for common ground.

William nodded, "You knew Sylvia too, I presume."

"Yes. Yes I did." Chaeronea whispered.

William waited a minute, hearing the soft hints of a secret trying to reach through Chaeroneas voice. He didn't want to pry, but he thought it better to ask her about it. Maybe she wanted to get something off her chest. "What to expand on that?" He asked her softly.

Chaeronea took a few deep breaths, trying to calm herself and the unusual wet tears starting to form behind her eyes. She didn't know this man in front of her but she did want someone to talk to. Sooner or later, with all the time she spent with Liam, it was all going to slip out. She might as well tell someone else so she didn't accidentally tell Liam first.

"Can you keep a secret?" She whispered, meeting his gaze. He nodded. "I think... I think I'm the one who killed her."

ooo

William and Chaeronea had moved to sit at the kitchen table and Chaeronea had her hands wrapped around a glass of water. She had managed to go the whole conversation without a single tear streaking her face. Her goal was to present the facts to him, measure his reaction, and see exactly how much she had messed up. She had already told him about her meeting with Clementine, about how she had given him the information about Liam and his life. She learned that William was a good listener but not very comforting. Instead of helping her to feel better about the things she was saying, he just kept asking her clarifying questions. Chaeronea didn't know if that was a good sign or a sign that he didn't have anything good to say.

They had been sitting in silence for a bit when Chaeronea spoke again, "I liked Sylvia-"

"Did you?" William asked, non-judgmentally.

"Yes, yeah," She said,thinking, "I mean, we weren't best friends or anything... I guess, well, we each thought the other hated us. But I'm not really friends with anyone." She shrugged, "I didn't know what the Chairman was going to do, I didn't know what I was doing, and I didn't mean to hurt her, but I also didn't want to get hurt..." His questions suddenly made her feel the need to defend herself and her heartbeat quickened as she tried to explain her actions.

William stood up to refill his own glass, "Clementine is evil. You didn't do anything wrong, you were scared for your life and did what you had to do to stay alive." He offered.

Chaeronea looked down, "Then why do I feel so guilty? And why do I feel like I can't tell Liam?" she asked softly.

"Maybe because you're scared he will think you did it on purpose, because of your history with Sylvia."

Chaeronea nodded, "He will. He thinks I hated her."

"No he won't, and no he doesn't. I haven't been around you two very long, but I have noticed how well you know each other. Even through that cold, rough, sarcastic mask you put on, Liam sees you. He is going to know you didn't do it on purpose. He hates Clementine as much as the rest of us, all the blame is on that man and that man alone."

"Cold, rough, sarcastic exterior, huh?" Chaeronea chuckled, questioning. She didn't want to talk about the rest of it.

"I didn't mean it as a bad thing necessarily, it's just that something must have happened to you to make you not trust people. What was that?" He asked, sitting back down.

She hesitated, "My dad used to be abusive." She said, gazing into the living room.

"Oh. I'm really sorry."

"Don't be, he got what was coming to him." She nodded.

"I want to be of some help, so here is what I'll tell you." William started, leaning back in his chair, "Sylvia and I got along the first time I met her. But when I was supposed to be there for her, I wasn't. I broke a trust, and I broke it badly."

Chaeronea gave him a questioning look from across the oak table.

"But, when I found her a week or so ago, she forgave me. I don't know why, and I didn't deserve it. I let her leave that church, I layed there awake trying not to be noticed so I didn't have to comfort her because I didn't know how, I was scared-" He choked on his own words, "What I'm trying to say is, if Sylvia can forgive me after ten years for something I purposely did, something that was my fault, Liam is going to forgive you for something that happened two weeks ago and wasn't even your fault. You didn't do anything wrong, Chaeronea." He said, meeting her eyes.

Chaeronea met his gaze and felt a tear fall down her face, the first one she had cried all day. "I'm still trying to convince myself of that." She whispered.

ooo

"Liam, we have to go." Chaeronea said, shaking Liam awake. Liam jumped up.

"What- what happened?" Liam asked, looking around the room.

"You fell asleep, and we let you because you haven't been sleeping well lately, but now we have to go. Tuesday night's meeting is going to start soon and that's when Clementine's time is up." She explained slowly, a confused look on her face in response to his shocked one.

"I get it, I get it." he said to stop her overexplaining, "I just had a weird dream." he put his elbows on his knees, resting his head in his palms.

Chaeronea nodded her head, understanding the impact a bad dream could have on you. William threw Liam's coat at him, "Here, put this on, the cold air will help you shake it off." William also understood, he had trouble sleeping for a few years after and during the Awakening.

Liam just nodded and put the coat on, lifting the hood over his head. William did the same, and Chaeronea wrapped a dark scarf around her neck. They walked down the concrete sidewalk sprinkled with spiderweb cracks. Chaeronea carried a bag around her shoulder with the files inside, refusing to leave them at her house; they all agreed they should be kept in close range. The walk didn't take very long. Since Chaeronea usually led Tuesday night meetings, she lived only a few blocks away.

When they got to the community hall they climbed the roped-off staircase to the dusty balcony and sat on the floor where they could barely see over the railing.

From the balcony Liam spotted where he and Sylvia usually sat. He was surprised to see only one empty seat; his. But then he realized how Sylvia's spot must have been given away since her death, and how under different circumstances, he might be down there introducing himself to someone brand new right now.

He also noticed the absence of Matilda's seat. He scanned the crowd for her but couldn't find a single trace of her blonde hair.

He sighed and Chaeronea gave him a questioning look, but he just shook his head, telling her to ignore it. They focused their attention to the stage as the room went silent and a large TV was wheeled in; Liam was already getting a bad feeling.

From between the balcony railings they watched as Clementine appeared on screen. They watched as he welcomed everyone and talked about the strength of their community.

From the balcony, they watched Clementine put a bounty on their heads.

From the balcony, they saw their community change in a new way. They watched the crowd become restless as they thought about getting the money he spoke of. Liam could only wonder if he had made his world worse in an attempt to make it better.

All he could do was watch, horrified, as Clementine explained the need for protection against threats, about rewards. His head filled with lies and propaganda until Chaeronea was pulling him away and William was fiercely whispering at him, but he couldn't hear them or process that they needed to leave. He was blinded by an anger that he had felt only once before; one that disabled him and left him dizzy.

He was rushed out of the town hall as quietly as possible while William and Chaeronea started to talk about a new hiding place for them. They tried calling after him but he kept walking so all they could do was follow him. His feet moved quickly down the sidewalk but he didn't worry about being seen, not just because everyone was in the brick building they had just left, but because his mind wandered to other issues.

As they walked, Chaeronea tried to think of something that could comfort him, something that could tear his gaze away from the sidewalk. Hundreds of sentences filled her mind but she couldn't bring herself to say anything, fearing it would all come out wrong.

They approached an old brick building with long, cracked columns in the front and old marble steps leading to the door. Liam knew the front would be locked, and so he walked around to the side of the building and climbed up the fire escape until he reached a glass window, and with Chaeronea and William behind him, he walked into the old abandoned library forgotten by everyone but Sylvia, who had spent hours pouring over the books left here. He was overcome by her presence and a feeling of failure, but taking deep breaths he sat down amid bookcases, out of sight from the outside, to figure out his next move.

CHAPTER SEVEN

Chaeronea hated the library.

It was dusty and moldy from age. She felt overwhelmed by the words and opinions stuffed into the leather and cloth backings. The floor creaked underneath her and she ran into spiderwebs wherever she turned.

But mostly, she hated the look of hurt on Liam's face as memories resurfaced.

They sat on some old couches that were clean, according to Liam, because Sylvia had come in and cleaned them one day. William seemed nervous, and Chaeronea was visibly uncomfortable, but she felt a little better sitting next to Liam on the purple upholstered couch. William sat across from them on a blue chair, watching the two.

"I'm sorry Liam, I thought he would comply." Chaeronea sighed.

"I didn't." Liam replied honestly, "I mean, I guess I hoped for it, but I knew it was never going to happen. Clementine is just too dark. He doesn't understand the value of human life, or rights, or anything like it."

"Liam's right, we stole the files for a reason. We all knew this would happen, we just wanted to avoid it. We wanted to play nice-" William added.

"But Clementine doesn't play nice." Liam finished.

They all hesitated.

"I guess we should look at the file then." Chaeronea offered, and she pulled the beige envelopes out of her bag, tossing hers, Liam's, and Williams on the ground and opening up the last one.

"You up for this?" She whispered to Liam, and he nodded at her without meeting her gaze. Chaeronea took a deep breath before starting to read, "Ryan Smith, 43. White hair, glasses. 6 foot 1."

"Wait." Liam interrupted, "What's his name again?" he asked hesitantly.

"Ryan Smith."

"Where is he from?"

"Long Island. Why?"

"Just, just wait. How old was he when he killed all those people?"

Chaeronea flipped through the pages, "23."

Liam did the math in his head, and all the breath left him. His pulse quickened and he could hear his heart beating inside his ears. He dizzly got up and walked to a bookcase, running his hand through his hair.

"Liam, what is it?" Chaeronea asked.

"You look like you've seen a ghost." William added.

Liam sunk down against the bookcase and William and Chaeronea kneeled in front of him. Chaeraona could feel the dusty carpet on her hands but she tried to ignore it. Liam put his head in his hands to try and get the room to stop spinning and his head to stop pounding. Several minutes passed, and all that was heard was his breathing.

"My name is Liam Wood. I am twenty years old. I live in this community and I started my life as a Witness two months after the Awakening ended. According to The House, there was nothing before that day, when I started as a Witness. But we know that can't be true because I'm twenty, not seven."

"Liam I don't understand-"

"Would you just *stop* talking, Chaeronea?" Liam asked quietly but sharpley, and Chaeronea's eyes met the floor. "My name is Liam Wood. But before that day, my name was Liam Smith. I lived on Long Island, and my mom had me when she was 22." Liam spoke slowly, hearing himself, processing, "She had me when she was 22. My dad would have been 23, but he left when my mom found out she was pregnant."

Chaeronea gave Liam a questioning look, William took a deep breath; anticipating. Liam couldn't meet anyone's eyes, and he stared directly at the wooden floor beneath him.

What he said next didn't come out with shock or wonder. He spoke it as a fact, and a fact alone, void of any emotion to how attached he felt. "That means, the man who killed Sylvia, is my father."

CHAPTER EIGHT

Sylvia was 16, and she got sick.

It was just a cold. Liam and Matilda both knew about it, they both wanted her in bed, they both wanted her to drink fluids and sleep it off, but Sylvia wouldn't admit she was sick. Through the sniffling and the coughing and the sweating she still went to all her classes, assemblies, and activities.

"Sylvia, just go to bed, you're exhausted." Liam nudged her. They were sitting on a white couch in the common room, Sylvia's legs across his lap, her head on his shoulder. Matilda was sitting across from them in a black armchair.

"No I'm fine, it's too early anyway." She mumbled, trying to keep her eyes open.

"It's not *that* early." Matilda tried, realizing that it would be at least two more hours until she herself went to sleep.

"It's fine, I'm fine. What were we talking about again?"

They continued their conversation until a few minutes later when Matilda was called away by another friend. Liam nudged Sylvia again. She groaned and shifted in place, curling more into his chest. He laughed a bit, "Why won't you just admit you're sick?" He asked lightly.

She pushed her hair behind her ear, "C'mon Lee, you've read the dictionary. A human is a person who is in good health, always."

"So you're afraid that being sick makes you less human?" He asked, confused.

"No, Liam. Let's say I was sick, hypothetically." She curled her sleeves around her hands, "In The House, people don't get sick, philosophically. Everyone is supposed to be healthy, and if you aren't, we don't know what happens. Look around, you don't see anyone here with cancer, or broken bones, or mental disabilities. They're trying to create a perfect human existence, without illness and sickness and brokenness."

Liam looked around the common room at the different faces. Sure, there were different races and ages and sizes, but for the first time Liam realized that there was no one unhealthy. He felt odd, like he was a guinea pig someone was looking in on; that someone could change his surroundings however they wanted, and sometimes he might not even notice.

So Liam understood Sylvia. They both knew that The House had sick policies, and that if you had a cold, you could be excused from classes for a certain time period. But Sylvia didn't want to be watched. What if she didn't get better after the designated week? What if The House decided to classify her as someone who gets sick a lot? Would she be considered weaker? Would they take her just because she was now on their radar?

Being anonymous was the name of the game, and Liam and Sylvia played together.

ooo

Clementine was his name.

Tarrence Jonah Clementine, but no one knew that part, and he didn't want them to.

He was Chairman Clementine to everyone. Or just Chairman, but never just Clementine. It was a matter of respect. The fact that his name had no meaning other than a small orange pulpy fruit, the fact that his last name was more than four letters, all of it showed how much more important he was then everyone else.

And he truly believed it.

Clementine's biggest pet peeve was being disrespected. So when Liam Wood and all of Clementine's patrol men came marching in, threatening him, Clementine did not appreciate it. Granted, he started it, but he would never admit that.

He's the Chairman, if he wants something, it happens, and what he wanted was to have Liam, Chaeronea, William, and the other patrol men under his control. He did *not* want to take the deal. So he went a little old fashioned and put a bounty on their heads; he had everyone working to get them.

He sat on the couch in the living room of his penthouse apartment, looking over the community, when Ryan walked in.

"Only working elevator in this community." He grinned, strolling out of the elevator, "I need one at my house, getting too old for stairs." He said, walking over to the couch across from Clementine and casually sitting down. Clementine didn't look impressed at Ryan's familiarity.

"This is not a social call, Ryan. I have some news." Ryan's face grew grave and he leaned his elbows on his knees. "Your son came to see me today."

Ryan ran a hand through his white hair. "He's trouble."

"He's been trouble his whole life. He's just like you."

Ryan scoffed, "No he's not. He's soft. That girl made him soft."

"She was the only one there for him, according to Chaeronea."

Ryan got defensive, "There for him through what? There for him as the world got better? Come on Clementine, you're talking as if you don't believe in your own fucking philosophy! The world you created!" He got up and paced in front of the couch, running his hand through his hair. "Who is Chaeronea anyway? Your inside girl?"

"Yes, except not anymore, she's turned against us." Clementine stayed calm.

"Of course." Ryan ran his hand through his hair again.

"I think she likes him."

"Everyone likes my son, Clementine. He gets that from his mother. But why are we even talking about this? Are you going soft on me too, Clementine?"

"It's just that I've been thinking about what your boy said. If I died, I'd want people to remember me, to mourn me."

"You *are* going soft Tarrance! Get your fucking act together."

"Clementine. *Chairman* Clementine."

Ryan's hands turned to fists, "Yes, exactly, Chairman! You are the Chairman of all the communities all around the world, don't you get it? If you want people to mourn your death, you have that power. But you can't go changing these rules that already exist for *commoners*, or we risk questioning. And what's The House's rules on that?"

Clementine sighed, "Questioning is an outdated word in times like these, for when we all live harmoniously, un-chaotically-"

"There is no need to throw around ideas of other possibilities, classification works, and it is all how it should be." Ryan finished, "Exactly. Get it together, you built this, you can't start tearing it down."

"We built it. Don't pretend you don't have your ideas in here too."

Ryan sighed and went to sit next to Clementine, "We're a team, Clementine. A team. And in a team everyone has to pull their weight, that means you can't go soft on me."

Clementine shook his head, his eyes scanned his blue colored room. Sylvia Blue, her last name had been Blue. He closed his eyes, feeling his head sway, why was this starting to affect him now?

"So what do we do?" He breathed.

"We fight back. We continue to spread our dream. That humans can be-"

"At peace with themselves and others, and therefore live harmoniously together on the Earth. Yes, I know the dream." Chairman Clementine sighed.

"Good."

○○○

"We have to *talk* about this."

"I don't think he wants to talk-"

"This is huge, we can't not address the elephant in the room."

"Chaeronea he *doesn't want* to talk."

"So what? We let him bottle it all up? How is that healthy?" Cheaeronea yelled back at William.

"What's our goal?" Liam spoke up, turning away from the window he was previously staring out of, and Chaeronea and William stuttered to answer his question. "I mean, think about it. I wanted to avenge Sylvia's death because I wasn't allowed to mourn her publicly. I wanted her life to matter and so I started this crusade. But what's the point now? I didn't want to start a revolution, I didn't want to overthrow Clementine. I can't run a whole community, *multiple* communities! Maybe this was just my own weird way of grieving instead of trying to make a difference. I threw myself into it because I needed something to throw myself into, instead of the pathetic hole of sadness I'm feeling. I started something that I can't finish, that I don't know how to finish, that I don't know if I *want* to finish."

Everyone felt the beat of silence, and then Chaeronea burst out laughing.

"Chaeronea!" William said shocked.

"I'm sorry, I'm s-s-sorry, really." She said through laughter, "But listen to him. This is ridiculous!"

Liam walked across the room to the couch, hurt. He had meant what he said. He hung his head and waited for Chaeronea to get a hold of herself, "Liam. L-Liam, wait. I don't mean to be mean or anything, it's just-" She took a deep breath to stabilize herself and then sat down next to him, "It's just that you've always know what you've wanted Lee-"

Liam shot her a look, his gaze piercing her eyes. "Liam." She corrected. "Maybe you did start this from a place of pain, a pain that is real, and that I understand," She placed her hand on his shoulder, "But deep down, you always wanted to know... well, in the end, you always wanted to know who killed the women you were in love with. Just like how before the Awakening, if someone was killed, their family wanted justice for their death. You wanted it to be recognized, you wanted *her* to be recognized, because her life was precious, and special, and unique. Because you loved her." Liam nodded, silent tears slipping down her cheeks, a heavy weight on his shoulders he didn't know if he wanted to bear. "And we stood by you Liam, because we believe, we honestly believe in what you wanted for Sylvia. We believe it, and we want it for everyone living here. So I'm going to say this: maybe you're not ready to fight off Clementine, or face your father. Maybe you aren't ready to re-design communities, but we're going to take it one step at a time, together. Because yes, you have started something, and that something is going to be finished, because it is a cause worth fighting for."

William had left to give them privacy, and Liam found himself staring at Chaeroneas gray eyes. He nodded his head, "Okay."

She let out a breath she didn't know she was holding, "Okay," She repeated back to him.

ooo

William had seen a lot of things in his 44 years of life.

Sunrises. Sunsets. Births. Deaths. Bombings. Destruction. The ocean at midnight. Hundreds of combat boots tied to trees. Double rainbows. Cults of people living underground. Cars stacked on top of each other to form walls. Fields of rock sculptures; a lot of crazy things.

But never, in his 44 years of life, his 22 years of comfort and bliss, his 2 years of combat, all his training, all his work, had he seen so much yarn.

136 balls of yarn.

"Yeah... Sylvia liked to knit, so she collected any yarn she could find, since they don't make it anymore." Liam explained, gesturing around the basement of The House he used to share with Sylvia, "When the neighbors heard, they brought her any yarn they could find because Sylvia was always so nice to them. Mr. Alvarez down the street works in the Awakening Clean-Up department, most of it came from him."

William took a deep breath, "Wow."

"Wow." Chaeronea added.

"Yeah. Now all we have to do is get it out of here." Liam shrugged.

"Right, because it's that easy." Chaeronea glared sarcastically.

"Hey now," Liam replied, smiling, "It won't be that hard, we can roll it out."

"Roll? They're balls of yarn Liam. Use your brain, how do you think that is going to go?" Chaeronea rolled her eyes.

"Well I mean we can tie the yarn to one end, and then that way it won't unravel-"

"You want us to tie the ends of 136 yarns? While we are in a house targeted by the hundreds or people looking for us?"

"Okay well when you put it like that-"

William started to laugh, Chaeronea put her hands on her hips, staring him down. She was wearing a pair of high waisted black jeans and a black long sleeve to blend into the night. Her hair was up in a bun and she felt gross because she hadn't showered since before sneaking into Clementine's office. Liam was thinking, wearing jeans and a dark blue long sleeve. He pushed his hair out of his face.

"What?" Chaeronea asked William annoyed.

"Nothing, nothing. You two are just- adorable." William said honestly, shrugging. Chaeroneas face turned a dark shade of red and Liam gave her a sideways glance and a smile, "Anyway, no need to worry. The patrolmen are staying with one of my friends who actually lives right down the street. I can go get them, they can help with the yarn. And it's really dark outside, no one will see."

Liam and Chaeronea agreed and then waited while William left to get everyone.

"This is quite a plan you have, Liam Wood."

Liam flinced, remembering when Sylvia used his last name. "Yes. Yes it is Chaeronea... Chaeronea..." Chaeronea gave him a sideways glance. "I don't know your last name."

"No, you don't." She smiled.

"How is that even possible?" He exclaimed. Liam was sitting against the cold concrete wall with his arms on his knees. Chaeronea went to sit next to him, and she crossed her arms over her chest to keep them warm. She wouldn't admit it, but the basement was cold. Sitting next to Liam, she felt odd. Usually, before Sylvia's death, it was a comfort to be around him. But now, she just felt guilty. The cold from the floor seeped up through the bottoms of her feet, crawling through her blood. The moment was light, but she suddenly felt heavy. Her last name was just another secret she was keeping from him, and in those few seconds she felt her breath hitch; trying desperately to get air into her lungs she inhaled quickly and her eyes started to well with tears because she couldn't keep doing this to him. She didn't know how she felt, but she knew that she was hurting him, even if it was indirectly.

Liam noticed, "Chaeronea, it's fine. It's fine! I don't need to know!" He assured her, "What's wrong?" But she couldn't speak, she choked on her own panic attack and Liam grew even more concerned. "Breathe with me, it's okay. Close your eyes. In, out. In, out." He wrapped his arms around her, rocking her back and forth. He didn't know how he felt, but he knew he couldn't let Chaeronea be hurt.

When she caught her breath, he leaned back and grabbed her wrists in a comforting way, but

Chaeronea couldn't help but flinch. He raised an eyebrow at her, and more tears began to slide down her cheeks. Liam moved his other hand to her right wrist, slowly pulling down her sleeve. With Chaeronea shaking her head, Liam saw her half-inch scar.

"Chaeronea," He whispered, "What happened?" He gazed at her, struck, "Why?" He breathed out.

She took a deep breath, "Liam, there's something I've been keeping from you." She whispered.

They were facing each other, and he put his hands on the sides of her face, wet with tears; Liam noticed there was something so powerful about contact through a person's tears, like a part of their soul is out in the moment for you to touch, gently, not to hurt. She was exposed in front of him, and he wanted her to feel safe. They learned their heads together, and Chaeronea closed her eyes; now was her chance.

"What is it?" He asked softly

"When you asked me how things went with Clementine, I lied." She started.

"Okay."

"Clementine, he threatened me."

"Chaeronea, I'm- I'm so sorry. That must have been-"

"No." She cut in, shaking her forehead against his, "No. Don't be sorry, just- don't." Liam stayed silent, he didn't want to push. Instead, he tried to make his presence welcomed, so that she would feel comfortable telling him the rest. She tried to push it away, she tried to push him away, because she felt she wasn't worth enough to be in his embrace. But as much as she tried, and wanted to, they were like magnets that couldn't be separated.

"He told me, he told me that I would be safe, and that you would be safe, if I informed on you." A tear slipped from her cheek and fell onto his jeans.

"What- what does that mean?" He whispered.

"It means that, on the night before Sylvia died." She took a deep breath, "On the night before Sylvia died, I got a call from Clementine, and he asked me questions, about you, and your life, and..."

"And what Chaeronea?" Liam asked more forcibly, leaning against her.

"And Sylvia." She whispered. When Liam didn't talk, she went on, "About who she was, and how important she was to you." But Liam stayed silent, holding her arms, his forehead against hers. "Liam. Please, say something." She whispered, her voice shaking, barely audible. "I'm so, so sorry."

Liam took a few shaky breaths, he kept his eyes closed, he felt Chaeronea's pulse underneath his hands. He took his time, ten minutes, maybe more, before he finally spoke. "You have nothing to be sorry about." He said firmly.

That's when Chaeronea lost it.

Streams of tears started to run down her face as she shook her head back and forth, "No, no, no, Liam you don't *get it*." She tried firmly. Her hands started shaking and her hair started to fall out of her bun onto her face, sticking to her face. "I *killed* Sylvia, I *killed her*." Chaeronea tried to get out of Liam's grip, tried darting her eyes away, but Liam wouldn't let her go, he pulled her against him as she kept choking out, "You don't get it. You don't get it. You should be yelling, you should hate me."

"Stop. Chaeronea." He could feel her shaking against him, "Stop." Liam grabbed Chaeronea by the shoulders and made her look him in the eye. Her eyes were glassy and she kept squirming but Liam held her still, starting to cry himself, "I *know* who killed Sylvia. My *father* killed Sylvia. Ryan Smith killed Sylvia. And Clementine told him to do it. You didn't kill Sylvia. *You* didn't shoot her. Because listen to me, *listen* to me Chaeronea." Liam let go of her, and moved his hand to her chin, moving her face to meet his eyes again. "You are a lot of things, Chaeronea.

Smart? Yes. A leader? Very much. Annoying? Absolutely." He gave her a weak smile, "But a killer? No. Not at all. You didn't do *anything* wrong."

They rested their foreheads together again, "Don't you dare think you did," he whispered, running his thumb over her scar.

CHAPTER NINE

By 5am, all the yarn had been moved to Central Park. Liam and Chaeronea sat on the sidewalk with the patrol men sitting nearby.

"This isn't going to work." Liam breathed.

"Yes it will, trust yourself." Chaeronea assured.

Liam nodded his head and fidgeted with his hands, his hands that were capable of doing a lot of things. Recently, he had been wondering, why hadn't he been doing more with them? Once Chaeronea had confessed to him, all he could think about was getting his hands around Clementine.

But Sylvia wouldn't want violence, the voice in the back of his head told him.

He sighed, only one hour left before people started waking up, he could wait that long.

Before he knew it, Chaeronea was shaking him awake. An hour and a half had passed and he had fallen asleep. "Sorry, I let you sleep because I thought you might need it. And listen, if you want to talk about your... Ryan, we can."

Liam rubbed the sleep out of his eyes, "Thanks, but we should get to work." He put his hand out, and Chaeronea grabbed on, helping him up. He dusted off his jeans, looking around the park. He watched people leave their homes on their way to work, and William gave him a small nod, so Liam took a deep breath and spoke at the top of his voice, "My name is Liam Wood."

Fifteen people turned to look at him, whispers started circling, wondering if he really was *the* Liam Wood, the one with the bounty on his head. Some even ran off to get others. *Good,* Liam thought, *I need a crowd.*

He continued, "My name is Liam Wood, and when I was 12, I learned the value of a life." People started to inch closer, interested in what he was saying. "It's something that The House doesn't want you to know, because to them, we all are files, names, and numbers."

"We are our best school subject, our job, our height, our gender, our race. These are things that define us. Not if we are kind, or funny, or talented singers. Things totally out of our control define who we are. And when we die, no matter how we die or how we lived, we stop existing; in this world, in this community, and in people's memories. Or at least that's how The House wants it."

By this time a crowd started to gather and Liam had an audience, "When I was 12, I learned the value of a life. You all learned it to, at some point or another, but you've forgotten it, because The House wants you to.

"Ten years ago, the world we knew, the world we grew up in, the world we wanted to raise families in, ended. And look, I'm not denying we have a pretty good life. We all thought living in dystopia would include zombies or radioactive gas or something like that. We have food on the table, jobs, clothes, we can breathe fairly clean air. It's not so bad, is it?"

The crowd murmured, "But we are missing something. The House wants us to be classified, because they think that will make everyone happy. *Knowing* yourself is supposed to make you happy, according to them. But how can we be happy if we don't know the worth of our own life, of everyone's life.

"Let me give you a quick history lesson, stories that The House has pushed from your memory. In 1920, Women fought in peaceful protest to be able to vote, and it was granted. In 1965 a law was based that said you can't be excluded from voting because of your race, after African Americans had been working for *centuries* to be able to vote in the country they lived in and worked in. Do you even remember what voting is? No, because for our whole 'Witness' lives," Liam air-quoted, "Clementine has been in power. Voting is when the people choose who rules over them. Voting is another way to show the value of life, and that's why people fought to do it for so long. When you vote, you take a minute of your life to give value to another person's life. *That's* how special your life is, it has *that much* power."

Liam expected blank stares but was surprised when he saw people shaking their heads in agreement. Maybe he wasn't crazy. Maybe Sylvia was right, maybe they all felt this way, maybe they were just too scared to say it out loud. Maybe his plan would work.

Maybe.

"But this isn't about voting. Or maybe it is, but it's about so much more too. Clementine lives right up there," And Liam turned to point at a skyscraper that overlooked the park. "He is probably sitting up there right now, and we are going to do exactly what those people in history did all those years ago. We are going to do a peaceful demonstration against The House's idea that our lives have no value, because they do. We all deserve to be heard, and when we pass, we deserve to be respected for the lives we led."

"So, come gather around, and make a circle in this clearing. Everyone needs to be in this." More and more people had started to gather, forgetting about the job they needed to be at in five minutes. Men and women gathered to form the circle Liam was talking about, and Liam was shocked, because he had not expected it to work. Chaeronea just flashed him a big smile, she always knew, because she knew the value of his life.

"Perfect, perfect. Let everyone in. We want Clementine to see us. Okay, perfect. This is something the love of my life once told me about, something she had done before the Awakening. I'm going to start, and you'll have to speak loudly so everyone can hear you. I have a ball of yarn here, and I'm going to hold onto one end of it, and pass the ball to someone I appreciate. And when I do that, I'm going to say why I appreciate them, because everyone needs a little reminder of this. We are going to keep going, and when the yarn runs out we'll just tie more on."

Liam held onto one side of a blue ball of yarn and started unravelling a couple feet of it as he spoke, "We are going to create a web, and Clementine is going to see it all the way up there in his penthouse. It's going to show just how connected and united this community is. It's going to show how without one of us, the web would collapse. It's going to show that each and every one of our lives matters.

"I'll start," Liam scanned the circle, even though he already knew where she was, "I want to appreciate Chaeronea. Throughout all of this, everything that has been happening the past week, you have always been there for me. Thank you Chaeronea." Chaeronea turned a color she hoped Liam wouldn't notice and reached out to grab the ball of blue yarn that was flying towards her. When she did, her and Liam were connected by a single thread of blue wool, but it felt like more.

Chaeronea appreciated William, who appreciated one of his fellow patrolmen, who appreciated his neighbor, who appreciated the local deli man, and it went on and on. When the yarn ran out, they did exactly what Liam said and tied on another color. Blue turned to primary red, red to dark purple, purple to rusty yellow and then yellow to neon green.

They connected themselves, physically, in hopes that above them, Clementine could see how connected they were emotionally, and how much that connection meant to each and every citizen there.

CHAPTER TEN

"We could kill-"

"I told you, *no more deaths*." Clementine urged again.

Ryan put his fist to the table, "There is no other way to solve this."

"Well, your son is the one who caused this, so if you're suggesting death-"

"Clementine, we have an agreement." Ryan said sternly.

"Yes, yes we do; immunity for the boy. But every person in this community is the son or the daughter of someone else in this community, don't you see that?"

"The labels of 'mother' and 'father' don't even exist. If a child is born we take them right to the school, they don't get raised with parents. Why am I even explaining this to you? It was *your* fucking design!"

"I understand that!" Clementine stood up, raising his voice. "But your kid got into my head! We can't go around killing people to fix the problem because if we do, their loved ones will feel the same way you do when I mention killing your son! How can you just be okay with making someone feel that way?!"

"I don't love him." Ryan blinked.

Clementine raised an eyebrow, "How can you say that? After all the years you've spent watching him, working for me in exchange for his immunity, you're telling me you don't love him?"

"I wanted to protect him, but I don't want to deal with love. Love makes people weak, love ties people down. Love makes people make decisions that-"

"Impact people for the rest of their lives! Decisions are bad! People need a trusted person to make decisions for them blah blah blah. Yes, I've heard the speech!" Clementine waved his hands.

"Well it's all true and you know it. This is why we work together, because you know the normal human is dumb. They make decisions that impact everyone's lives and then they complain because they aren't happy. They don't know how to be happy."

"Look, I know you're an experienced killer and all who could probably take me down right now, but remember that *I'm* the one who runs this community. *I* call the shots, *I* protect your son. I started this all with a crusade, I got us here. I dropped the bombs, I started the wars. This community is based on *my* ideas. So don't you dare try to take my community away from me."

Ryan nodded his head, "I know, I know. I'm just saying that-"

"No. I created this *whole world* because I wanted my people to have rights."

"You mean your terrorist organization."

Clementine gave Ryan a look, and Ryan just raised his hands in fake surrender, "I wanted them to have rights. I wanted them to be happy, and the only way for that to happen is for them to know themselves. They were lost souls. They needed to be told who they were" Clementine started to pace, and when he passed the window he paused, doing a double take and walking back to the window because he saw something unusual; A giant, multicolored yarn web. Tons of community members were forming the circle, and it continued to grow as more people arrived. Clementine put his hand on the windowsill, growing angrier by the second. "You see, *this* is my problem. I let little insignificant people get into my head and start changing what I've worked for. Come look at this, your son is probably the cause of this, some sort of show against me. Can you believe this? After everything I've worked for, I have to deal with this." Ryan came beside him, shaking his head and holding two glasses. Clementine was the only one who owned liquor in the community, and Ryan took advantage of it when he could, "What's this for?" He asked, surprised.

"Clementine, with everything that's going on right now, I think it's important we take a minute to just look and appreciate what you've done. You're right, *you* created this, all by yourself. You got everyone to believe in your beliefs, and a couple people aren't going to change that. We will take care of it." Ryan smiled, handing the crystal glass filled with dark red liquor to Clementine, patting him on the back.

"Wow. Thank you. To the community that *I* built." Clementine clinked his glass to Ryan's and then drank the bitter liquid.

"And, to no more killing." Ryan sneered, sipping his drink.

When Clementine's glass hit the floor, Ryan didn't even flinch.

As Clementine gasped for breath, sinking to the ground, Ryan squatted down in front of him, "That was always your problem, Tarrence." Ryan said, setting down his drink on the light, now wine stained wood floor next to him. Clementine tried making a sound, asking what had happened, but only puffs of air left his mouth, "Sh, sh. Don't try to talk, just listen. I want this to be the last thing you hear.

You always were so, what's the word? Impressionable. You used to be so strong during the Awakening, and then you started going soft a long time ago. When the war was over you thought you could relax. That was your mistake, people started getting ideas. My son, that girl of his, even me. But I was always there whispering into your ear, and maybe that's why you questioned yourself so much, because your best ideas, well, they were mine." Ryan smiled his devious smile as Clementine tried to reach out to hurt him, to protest, but he didn't have the strength. "All these years, I was just waiting for something like this to happen. And now that it is, well, you can see what's happening. I'm going to take this community over and do it right. People will learn that their decisions have consequences. My son will learn that his decisions have consequences. He will be raised right."

Clementine's face tightened in anger but there was nothing he could do, Ryan continued, "Tarrence, you will die knowing that in the next couple days, you will be forgotten."

And with one last struggling breath, Tarrence Jonah Clementine got in his last spiteful words, "Sylvia's. Not. Dead."

Part Three

"The fault, dear Brutus, is not in the stars, but in ourselves"

William Shakespeare, *Julius Caesar* I.ii.140-141

CHAPTER ONE

Clementine was out the window as soon as the words left his mouth.

Ryan's hands left Clementine's shirt collar as he felt the glass break around his hands. Glass shattered towards his feet and up near his face. He felt a sharp cut on his cheek but he didn't pay too much attention to it. Instead, he watched as the Chairman's body fell forty stories to the ground below.

He watched him land right outside of Liam's yarn circle, but he didn't have time to watch the citizens' first reactions. Ryan had already disappeared from sight, walking to the elevator as Liam's eyes went up to the window above, the empty wooden outline of a window raining glass.

When Liam made eye contact with Chairman Clementine's empty eyes, Ryan was in the elevator, tapping his foot.

Chaeronea put her hand up to her mouth. She couldn't move. The yarn circle started to unravel as people dropped their yarn. There was a cry, someone started to sob. This was their Chairman.

The elevator reached the first floor and Ryan's steps across the lobby echoed through the whole building. Outside, people were frantic. They whispered and speculated with wet eyes. They cried regret because they had never wanted death.

When Ryan started walking across the park, Liam didn't notice. He kept his eyes on the Chairman. A small part of him knew he'd have to look up eventually, face the man who had caused so much damage in his life. But for the moment, he couldn't move his gaze. In the eyes of the Chairman, Liam saw his revolution die. He felt hushed whispers, scared whispers. If this had happened the first time they tried a peaceful protest, what would happen the next?

Liam felt his presence before he saw him, and even though it made no sense, it felt familiar, as if a piece of him had been waiting for him his whole life. And Liam thought that maybe, that scary thought was true.

When Ryan was in sight of the crowd some started to turn to run. Others stayed, people frozen by their fear, or ones who wanted to hear the showdown in the midst of the chaos. Who, like Liam, could not tear their gaze away.

Ryan stood on one side of Clementine and Liam stood on the other. Liam didn't take his eyes off the body in front of him, "Of course it's you." He shook his head, "It's always you. This is what you do, isn't it? Some dad's grill in the backyard. Some toss the ball. Other's make model airplanes. But you kill people." Liam scoffed, still not meeting his eye.

"Look at me." Ryan spoke, sternly.

Liam continued to shake his head, "This is going to sound so fucking cliche, but when I imagined my long lost daddy, he was an astronaut. A famous lawyer. Someone who did good in the world. I thought that if you were helping people, then that was an okay excuse for you leaving."

"But I am helping people." Ryan said blankly.

Liam tapped his hand on his thigh, he felt himself shaking, and for the first time he met his father's eyes; the man he wanted to kill. "What *happened* to you?" Liam hissed, "What happened to make you like this? Were you abused as a child? Forgotten? Didn't anyone ever teach you right and wrong?"

"I know right and wrong."

"Right," Liam laughed, his anger crushing the syllables, "That decisions are *bad,* right?" He emphasized, "That we can't trust ourselves to make our own decisions because we influence others lives too much. So, let me ask you something, Mr.Perfect, who gave you the power to be that person who makes decisions for us? Who told you your decision about *killing* the love of my life was okay?"

Ryan looked like he wanted to argue, to defend his points, but something stopped him. He didn't know why he said what he did, maybe it was an olive branch, or maybe he hoped to see the look on Liam's face, but whatever reason it was, Ryan said, "Well, Sylvia might be alive."

Ryan watched all the color drain from Liam, all the fight, and Ryan almost forgot whose side he was on.

ooo

Bring. Bring. Bring.

The telephone on Matilda's desk rang and she picked up the receiver, "Community 412, this is Matilda."

"Chairman Clementine has died." A robotic voice rang through, *"Please distribute the message and wait for further instructions."* And then the line went dead. Matilda heard more ringing. She looked around the office to see other people picking up their phones. She watched as their faces changed.

Matilda stared down at the receiver, and one voice rang through her head. Liam's.

"Excuse me!" Matilda said to the first person who walked past her desk, "I need to go back."

ooo

"Liam! Wait!" Chaeronea called out, running down the sidewalk to catch up to him.

"Can't talk right now Chaeronea, have something I need to take care of." He said hurriedly.

"Liam, wait." She said again, grabbing his arm and whisking him around. Liam tapped his foot, waiting expectantly he raised an eyebrow at her. "Listen," She spoke softly, "You need to be careful about this, it could be a trap. Just think about everything Ryan is capable of."

"Chaeronea, you heard what he said. Clementine told him Sylvia wasn't dead."

"Why would Clementine tell him that? And why would Ryan tell you?"

"Maybe Clementine suddenly grew a conscience and Ryan was extending an olive branch. I don't know Chaeronea! I don't have time for this." He started to turn away.

"Liam," Chaeronea started, walking around him to block his path. "That man just pushed the Chairman out of a forty story building and now you are blindly following him into a House building that you are completely unfamiliar with."

"So what are you saying? I shouldn't even *try* to look for her? She's the love of my life Chaeronea." Liam looked right into her eyes, and she suddenly didn't recognize this new, desperate Liam.

"I'm just saying you need to take a minute. You aren't in the right headspace, you aren't thinking clearly. Be careful, and on top of that, don't get your hopes up. If she's not there Liam, it's going to be even harder to lose her a second time." Chaeronea spoke slowly, putting her hand on his upper arm.

Liam shook his head, "I'm going." He said, pushing his way past her.

Chaeornea turned to watch him go. Ryan waited for him a few buildings ahead and the two kept their distance. Liam walked straight, determined.

Suddenly Chaeronea felt William's presence next to her. "There he goes." He whispered.

"Yeah," She breathed out, "I'm worried." She admitted.

"Me too." William added, "Let's pick up this yarn and head home. We're safe now that there isn't a bounty on our heads. We can wait for Liam there."

Chaeronea nodded her head and William placed a friendly arm over her shoulder, leading the girl away despite her eyes staying on Liam's disappearing figure for as long as possible.

ooo

"What do you mean I can't go back?" Matilda shouted across the counter.

"Ms., you just transferred. You can't just go back and forth switching. Under The House rules, you may switch once every five years."

"Five *years*?" Matilda asked, "I can't wait five years!"

"I'm sorry, these are the rules." The receptionist told her, "Do you have a problem with them?" She raised her eyebrow.

Matilda recognized a trap when she saw one and quickly closed her mouth. "No." She huffed, grabbing her bag.

As she left the transfer office Matilda wondered how she could escape the community she had desperately tried to get into.

CHAPTER TWO

"Where could she be?" Liam asked frantically.

Ryan met his eyes, shrugging.

Suddenly, Liam was on top of him, pinning him against the wall, "*Where* could she be?" He asked, inches from Ryan's face. "You do not want to mess with me right now. So tell me *where she could be.* You owe me that."

Ryan pushed Liam off in one fluid motion, "I *owe* you?" He asked shocked, "You have no idea how much I've done for you." He added, shaking his head, pointing his finger at Liam. "Did you ever stop to wonder why Clementine didn't just kill you when you published that article? Or when you made up that paper? It was because of me, I traded myself for *your* immunity. I don't owe you anything."

Liam ran his hand through his hair, "You have a messed up way of showing your love." He spit out.

"Love?" Ryan laughed, "Love? I don't love you boy. I protected you because you're blood, not out of love or the fucking kindness of my own heart. No, I protected you out of obligation. Don't flatter yourself."

"Oh, so I guess I should be thankful then!" Liam yelled, throwing his hands in the air, "After all, you did so much for me! Like, for example, killing the love of my life?"

"That girl was making you soft, made you doubt the system."

"The system is shit!" Liam yelled back, "Anyone in their right mind can see that, anyone who isn't brainwashed! But that's the problem, you're brainwashed, they got to you too." He shook his head.

"I have my own beliefs, I'm not a sheep who follows blindly like the rest of Clementines pack."

Liam stopped pacing, looking straight at Ryan, "So you made the decision to kill her on your own then?"

Ryan shook his head, slowly, "We needed a punishment, and you were off limits."

Liam laughed, "This is so messed up," he cried, "This world, this situation. You don't even regret what you did." He said earnestly.

Ryan looked him right in the eye, "Why would I?"

There was a minute of silence before Liam opened his bag to grab something. "Sylvia Blue was 5 foot, 4 and a quarter inches." He started, "She didn't like anything cherry flavored, but she loved real cherries."

"Why are you telling me this?"

"She didn't like choosing between cats and dogs because she liked them both equally; Just like science and the arts, just like the colors. Sylvia loved Shakespeare, and all languages, and would spend hours inventing new alphabets on strips of paper."

"Liam."

"She thought you had to spin the lemonade and pour it in the glass while it was spinning or else it wouldn't taste the same. She couldn't cook brownies to save her life. She liked to blow on the wishballs."

"Stop."

"No, I won't stop. Not until you realize that Sylvia Blue was a person, a human being. She had this amazing life, with a vibrant personality, and you took that away. You reduced her to this," Liam threw the copy of the newspaper he made at Ryan, the white haired man catching it and turning it to look at the front page. "You reduced all that vibrancy to black and white."

Ryan looked up at Liam, "The world is black and white."

"Not my world," Liam shook his head, "My world is blue."

ooo

Wallace laid on a blanket she had spread out under the stars. Sylvia was beside her, looking up at the sky.

"Where's William?" Sylvia asked.

"He got called into the base for something." Wallace sighed.

"Oh."

"Yeah." She whispered.

They laid together, staring up at the night sky, watching the pictures of warriors and animals dance above them.

"That one is Orion." Wallace pointed out.

"And that's the big dipper." Sylvia pointed to. "The fault, dear Brutus, is not in our stars, but in ourselves."

Wallace laughed, "Shakespeare?"

"Of course."

Wallace paused, "What do you think it means?"

"What?"

"The quote."

"Oh. Well, think of it in terms of horoscopes. You know? People check their horoscope to see if today is going to be a good day, a bad day, etc. The quote is saying that if you have a bad day, it isn't because of stars or horoscopes or fate or anything, it's because of yourself. Your own decisions."

"I thought so. Do you believe it?"

"In fate?" Sylvia questioned.

"Yeah. Well, no. About the decisions."

"Well, of course. The decisions you make can really impact people."

"Right, so what if the fault is not because of the stars or your own decision? What if it's because of someone else?"

Sylvia thought for a minute, "Then, I guess that person wasn't very considerate. But it was still *someone's* fault, not the stars."

"Yeah."

Wallace stayed silent, but Sylvia had a question this time, "What do you think happens when you die?"

"You stop breathing."

"Right, I know that part, but like, after."

"So, the afterlife?"

"Yeah."

"I don't know." Wallace started, "The Egyptians think that when you die you go to an afterlife, underworld sort of thing. This god weighs your heart, and if it's good you get to go on, and if it's bad then an alligator human eats it."

"Intense." Sylvia mused.

"Yeah."

"Well what do you think happens?"

Wallace paused, "I think it would be cool if you got to see all of your family. But I guess I haven't really thought about it. Why?"

"I guess I'm just curious."

"Well, what do you think about it?"

"I think we go to heaven."

"Even the bad guys?"

"I don't know."

"Me neither."

Sylvia took a minute, "Are you scared?"

"Of death?"

"Yeah."

Wallace took a deep breath, "No. Well, maybe a little. Are you?"

"Not of natural death, no. Like when I'm old. But there are so many things I haven't done yet. I'm not scared, it would just suck to die young."

"I feel you there."

"Thank you."

"But don't worry, neither of us are going to die young. We'll grow old together and be those two old rocking chair ladies."

Sylvia laughed, "Who said I want to be stuck on a porch with you in my old age?"

"Well, our husbands will be there too." Wallace added.

"Ah, okay. Well, that's tolerable then." Sylvia smirked, earning a loving punch from her sister.

○○○

Liam paced the hall of holding cells for the twelfth time, "Sylvia?" He cried out, "Sylvia, c'mon. You have to be here, you have to be alive!" He sunk down against one of the walls, "I need you to be alive."

Ryan appeared at the other end of the hall. Liam stood up, his eyes staying on the spot Ryan had come from, but no one followed his father down the hall. "Liam," He started, standing in front of him, "I have some bad news."

"No, I don't want to hear it. She's alive, I know she is."

"Liam."

"No."

"I've tracked down the man who was responsible for her body."

"No, Clementine said she was alive."

"Clementine was trying to get under our skin!" Ryan told Liam frantically, "He wanted to throw us off, mess with our heads before he died. He wanted revenge."

"*Our* heads?! Our? There is no 'our'. You don't care about me, and especially not her. YOU are the one who killed her, you killed her... And," Liam started to cry, warm tears down his cheeks. His fists unclenched themselves and his body began to shake. His anger drained, he had done enough yelling. He tried to catch his breath, "And she's really dead?"

Ryan nodded his head, "Yes. I saw her body today." And in a last attempt, he added, "I can take you to see her."

Liam couldn't stop shaking. His throat went dry and he nodded his head, yes.

ooo

When Liam saw Sylvia's body lying on a table in a cold room on level two, the first thing he thought of was the fact that today, he had seen two dead bodies in the course of two hours, and that was probably some kind of record.

Unless you fought in the Awakening, Liam realized.

Ten seconds later he was thinking about his Sylvia, lying on a table in a cold room on level two, and so he took his jacket off and put it over the thin sheet she was wearing, a reflex.

He was twelve. It had been a month since he met Sylvia. Everyone knew there was something between them, but they didn't talk about it. It was their first time at this, and what do you say when the world you live in really doesn't acknowledge dating? Were they even dating? Liam remembers smiling at her a lot, telling her things to make her laugh. Catching her glance across the room, always trying to sit right next to her.

But he needed to make a move, Sylvia was waiting for it.

They were out in the yard during outside time, sitting on the top of the slide. They were talking, but something kept tripping Sylvia up. She was shivering so much it hurt her speech pattern.

"Here, you're freezing." Liam told her, taking off his coat to give to her.

She pushed it away, "I don't get cold, don't worry-y." She smiled, "Plus, then you'd-d b-b-be cold."

Liam rolled his eyes, "Don't be so strong for a minute and take the coat." He smiled.

She blushed, thanking him for the coat, and wrapped it around herself; it smelled like him. She leaned on his shoulder, and later on, she walked in wearing his jacket, holding his head.

He thought that made it pretty clear what they were.

"I'm going to give you a minute." Ryan said, almost robotically, closing the door behind him.

Liam walked around the table, taking a seat on a swivel stool. He reached out to grab her hand, but it didn't feel right, it was cold.

"I don't know what to say." He admitted, "You don't feel like Sylvia. You don't look like Sylvia." He started to cry, silent tears that landed on his coat. "I don't want to remember you like this." He whispered. "I love you."

"Lee, what's wrong?" Sylvia laughed.

"Just nervous, that's all." He told her, swinging their hands together.

"Why? We're just going up to the roof. We've done this a thousand times. Why are you worried all of a sudden?"

He shrugged, "Good question," He nodded, trying to keep cool.

Sylvia gave him a sideways glance, smiling, "Okay then."

Sylvia continued to talk about random things as they went up the old stairs. Liam nodded along, distracted.

"Lee! You aren't listening to me!" She huffed, fake mad.

"Sorry V, it's just that, wait. Here." He opened the door at the top of the staircase.

Syvlia inhaled as she took in the candles on the rooftop with the blanket spread out in the middle. "Liam, what's all this?" She asked, wide eyed.

"I want to tell you something, Sylvia." He told her, leading her to the blanket. "When I first met you, I knew I loved you. Every part of you, inside and out. So what I want to say is, I love you Sylvia Blue. I love you."

Sylvia looked up at Liam, "I love you too, Liam Wood. To the moon and right back to our crazy world." She said without hesitation.

"To the moon, and right back to our crazy world."

CHAPTER THREE

Liam saw blackness, and he liked it that way.

He liked that the curtains were drawn. He liked the door closed. He liked the blanket over his head.

He liked wallowing in his own sadness.

He could almost hear Sylvia's voice in the back of his head, *C'mon Lee,* she would say, *You can't mope over me forever.*

"Yes I can." He said, surprised to hear his own voice. He curled into himself, trying to find tears, but instead found dryness.

And that made him feel worse.

Chaeronea didn't know Liam could hear them whispering outside his door about him. Granted, it was Chaeronea's house, so Liam couldn't really complain. But on the other side, he honestly did not want to have to acknowledge how nice and concerned they were being. He wanted to be mad at them, he wanted them to leave him alone.

So it was very frustrating when Chaeronea cracked open the door and slid herself into the room.

"Hey," she whispered, "Can I get you anything? Food? Water?"

Liam turned onto his other side, rolling away from her, "Chaeronea, I really want to be left alone right now."

Chaeronea didn't say anything for a few moments. Then Liam heard her footsteps across the room, and a dent in the bed beside him. She wrapped her arms around his body, and she felt him tense against her, but after a minute, he sunk into her arms.

"He just needs someone to be with him right now," She had told William earlier.

He had agreed, *"He probably hasn't even been sleeping, just laying in the darkness thinking and thinking. That isn't healthy."*

Minutes later, Liam's breath started to even out.

ooo

Chaeronea hesitantly snuck away from a sleeping Liam about an hour later. She sat down at the kitchen table and picked up the phone, but stood up once it started ringing, pacing the kitchen floor.

As it rang, William opened the front door and Chaeronea waved him in. He had been spending a lot of time at her house recently and had become comfortable there. He came in and got himself a glass of water, raising his eyebrows at Chaeronea and motioning to the phone. She held up one finger and answered the ladies voice on the other end, "Hello, this is Community Dispatch and Transfer, how can I help you?"

"Hello, this is Chaeronea Bode and I'm hoping you can tell me the community number of a certain graduate."

"I'm sorry but that's confidential information."

"Did I mention I'm Director of Communications in this community? Oh, and I know Chairman Smith personally." She smiled into the receiver.

"Let me get that number for you." The lady said.

"That's what I thought. The name is Matilda, I don't know the last name. But she just transferred."

"Here she is. Looks like she just got to community 412 a week and a few days ago. And, hm, this is interesting. She's requested a switch back."

"Well, was it granted?"

"No, she will have to wait five years before she can switch back."

"I want the request granted."

"Ma'am we can't do that."

"You can't? Well, I guess I better take it up with Chairman Smith. What did you say your name was again?"

The lady paused, "I'll send the request through."

"Thank you." And Chaeronea hung up the phone, smiling.

"Here I was thinking you'd gone soft for Wood." William started, "But looks like you've still got it."

"Don't underestimate me." She smiled, a blush creeping up her neck.

ooo

Ryan knocked on the door of Chaeronea's apartment hesitantly. When she opened the door, he was relieved it was her and not Liam.

Ryan tapped his hand on his thigh, "I came to see Liam." He stated, his eyes darting around, looking behind her into the house.

Chaeronea didn't move from the door, "He's not really taking visitors." She told Ryan. Ryan met her eyes, was it just him or did he hear sympathy in her voice?

"You mean he doesn't want to see me." Ryan asked, adjusting his glasses.

"No, he doesn't want to see anyone." Chaeronea told him slowly, as if those words were a secret she wasn't supposed to be sharing.

Ryan took that in, understanding, "Let me see him. I need to talk with him." He paused, "Please." The word sounded odd in his mouth.

Chaeronea's eyes scanned Ryan. He looked different, softer around the edges. She didn't feel fear surrounding him like the day she met him. Her eyes landed on his nervous hand on his thigh, a habit Liam had to, and decided to let him into The House, "He's in the bedroom. First door on the right." She told him, pointing down the hall. William's eyes went wide and he stood up from the seat he had on the couch, unsure of how to act. Ryan moved right past him to get to the door.

Ryan opened the door and went to stand at the foot of the bed.

Liam opened one eye, "Chaeronea let you in here?" He groaned.

"Yes."

"I *do not* want to see you."

"I know."

Liam sat up for the first time in days, "Then why are you here?"

Ryan took a moment, "I'm Chairman now." He started, "That means I need a right hand man, and you're my son."

Liam had to stop his jaw from dropping, "You want me to work for you?"

"With me, yes."

"No way. I can barely stand to look at you, I won't stoop to your level and work with you and your beliefs."

"Take some time to think about it," Ryan said, starting to walk out of the room. "Maybe you could rub off on me."

"Doubt it."

Ryan looked back at Liam before he left, "Don't underestimate yourself Liam. Look at this, we just had a civilized conversation. You never thought that was possible, did you?" And Ryan closed the door.

"I never thought a lot of things were possible," Liam whispered, leaning against the headboard.

ooo

Ryan closed the door behind him and looked out at Chaeronea and William.

"Well, I'm going to go now."

Chaeronea nodded her head, "Alright." She paused, "How'd it go?" She offered. William shot her a look.

"Not good, maybe better." Ryan told her.

Chaeronea nodded her head again, walking him to the door, "Well, congratulations, I assume."

Ryan stared at her blankly, "For what?"

"Becoming Chairman of course."

"Oh, of course. Well, thank you." He nodded, and walked off towards his own house.

Chaeronea closed the door and rested her back against it, William shot her a glare.

ooo

When Matilda knocked on the door, Chaeronea and William were whisper-arguing about having a serial killer, also known as Liam's father, in the house. When no one responded to Matilda's tenth knock, she went ahead and opened the unlocked door.

Matilda's eyes were drawn first to Chaeronea and then to William who sat across from her. "Am I interrupting something?" She asked shyly. Both heads shot up to see her.

"Matilda, hello." Chaeronea said, shooting William one last glare. "We met once, I'm Chaeronea." She stuck her hand out to the blonde girl.

"Yes, I remember." Matilda said, shaking Chaeronea's hand.

"And this is William." Chaeronea added, introducing him as Matilda moved to shake his hand.

"William, like, Sylvia's dead sister's fiance William?"

"That would be me." He weakly smiled, "Nice to meet you."

"Back at you. So, I guess it's important I know why I'm here. Where's Liam?" She asked, gazing around the room.

"About that, we should fill you in." Chaeronea started.

ooo

Matilda knocked on the bedroom door.

"Chaeronea, I *really* don't want to talk to you after you let Ryan in-" But Liam was cut off from his rant as Matilda opened the door slowly.

Standing there, Matilda came face to face with the fact that she had run away; from her grief and Liam's grief. She had tried to be there for him, but he didn't need her. He needed to hurt, and he needed Sylvia.

She hadn't known how to help him. She hadn't known how to stop him from crying at night, or in the shower, or when he woke up. She hadn't known how to expunge the darkness that seemed to loom over their house, even with the curtains open. She herself had found it hard to breathe, with so many reminders of Sylvia around her, but her hands would not move to throw any of them away. The place had become suffocating.

The two of them had been living in a dangerous circle, one that only ended in the pain of realization; realizing Sylvia was really, actually gone. So she left. Matilda told herself it was fine, that Liam had other people to talk to, to care for him. He had Chaeronea, and all his friends from the paper.

And now, sitting in front of her was Liam, and she was hit with how much her abandonment must have hurt him, even if she hadn't meant it to.

His dark black hair curled and flipped over at the top, and his striking blue eyes that met hers seemed hollow. Matilda took a step inside the room. How do you even start a conversation with the weight of the past surrounding you?

She adjusted her glasses and met Liam's gaze; for one moment, she was ten again, and he smiled at her.

"Hey." She whispered.

"Matilda." He smiled.

She walked towards him, "You must hate-" But before she could finish her apology, her self demeaning rant, Liam had gotten up from the bed and wrapped her in a hug. She froze in his arms. By this time, Matilda had him memorized: the way his hair fell, the way he held himself, the way he showed friendship. He hugged her like his life depended on it.

This was Liam, one of her best friends, and she hugged him back.

Liam let go, "It's really nice to see you." He breathed out.

"It's nice to see you too," Matilda nodded, "But, I wasn't expecting this reaction. I thought you would hate me."

"I could never hate you."

"But I left, I left when you needed me the most."

Liam thought about this for a minute, sitting down on the bed with Matilda following, "I was angry then, no one could do anything for me." He paused, "But you're here now."

"Yes." She spoke softly, nodding her head.

Liam paused, "How are you doing?" He asked.

Matilda nodded her head, "I'm getting by. You?"

He looked around at the ruffled bed sheets, the shoes thrown on the floor and the curtains closed tight, "Not too great." He sighed.

Matilda wrapped her arms around his neck, "We're here for you," She whispered in his ear,

"Whenever you're ready to come out, we're ready for you."

ooo

Liam laid alone on his bed, trying to consolidate his thoughts. He thought about getting up, about eating, about talking, but he couldn't make himself do any of it. He spoke into the dark room, "If your whole life is one person, what happens when they're gone?"

"Liam, I'm not your whole life." He heard a familiar voice speak.

Liam sat bolt upright. He moved his gaze to the corner of the bed where Sylvia sat.

And Liam scrambled off the bed towards the opposite corner.

"Sylvia?!" He ran a hand through his hair. She nodded. Chaeronea opened the door right behind him.

"Liam? What's wrong? I heard you scream." She asked.

Liam looked back and forth between Chaeronea and Sylvia. He realized Chaeronea didn't see her sitting on the bed. He thought he must be going crazy. "Nothing, I just stubbed my toe, that's all." He lied, his face white as a sheet.

"Oh, okay. Let me know if you need anything." And she closed the door.

Liam stared at Sylvia, "This isn't possible. You're dead."

"Yeah, I am." Sylvia told him.

"But, so, then, how?" He stumbled.

"I don't know." She shrugged, "But I'm here. Come over here and see." She patted the bed next to her. Liam hesitantly walked over to sit next to Sylvia, a foot away. "Lee," She smiled, "It's me, I'm not going to bite." And he moved closer.

"Can I touch you?" He asked.

"Yeah, I think so." She said, and he reached out to grab her hand.

"Wow."

"I know." She smiled.

"Sylvia, I missed you so much."

"I know," She smiled sadly, "I missed you too."

"Why are you here?" He asked.

"Maybe to remind you that you have more than just me."

"You are my world." He stressed.

"That's sweet Liam," She smiled up at him, "But I'm gone now. You have to focus on what you actually have, not what you've lost. Like your writing, your new friends. This new job opportunity."

Liam scoffed, "I can't take that job."

"Why not?"

"Because then I'd be working for the man who killed you! All my morals would be out the window."

"But Liam, he's also your father. And this way, you'd be on the inside. You could accomplish so much that way."

"I don't know V.

"Just think about it." She told him, and gave his hand a squeeze before she stood up.

"Where are you going?" He asked desperately.

"I have to go." She said simply, "I'll be back. But Lee, you need to get out of this room. You can't just sit here all day in the dark."

"I know. But please, don't go. I can't lose you again." He told her, rushing up to her.

She touched his tear stained cheeks, "You aren't losing me Liam, I'm always here." She told him, touching his chest. His gaze went down to her hand, and when she disappeared, he sat down on the floor, looking at the spot where she was just standing.

CHAPTER FOUR

Liam opened the door and the light from the living room hurt his eyes. He put his hand up to block the light as Chaeronea, William, and Matilda came into focus.

"I need to talk." He stated.

"Okay, let's talk in here." Chaeronea started, leading him to the living room.

"What's up, Lee? You look like you've seen a ghost." Matilda told him.

"I have." He answered, meeting her eyes. "I saw Sylvia." Liam told them, stunned.

"Like, a photo?" Matilda asked hesitantly.

Liam shook his head, slowly. "She was sitting on the edge of the bed. She held my hand, and talked to me." Liam whispered, almost to himself.

"That's... new." William added.

There was a pause, "Is she here now?" Chaeronea asked, looking around the room.

Liam shook his head, "She left, but she'll be back. I know it."

"Is that a good thing?" William asked him.

Liam tilted his head, "I don't know" He looked around the room, like he was seeing it for the first time, slowly meeting Chaeonea's eyes. "I'm not broken." he said to her.

"I know." Chaeronea added, rubbing his back.

"I just miss her." Liam whispered.

"I do too, Lee." Matilda told him.

He ran a hand through his hair, "But you aren't seeing her like some crazy person."

Matilda thought for a minute, "No, I'm not seeing her. But I still see her Liam, in a different way. I see her when I make tea. I see her in every doodle I draw on my notepad at work. I think of her every time I see the color blue. I miss her too Lee, we all have different ways of going through that."

Liam nodded, getting up to walk to the kitchen, getting himself a glass of water. Chaeronea followed him. "I'm not broken." He repeated when they were alone, while she nodded, "Please don't leave. You can't leave. You're the only one who's ever stayed."

Chaeronea nodded, "I'm not leaving." She told him, "I promise."

ooo

Liam was eating a sandwich at the kitchen table, the first food he had had in days. Chaeronea had gone to take a shower and Matilda was out for fresh air. William did some dishes at the kitchen sink, whistling to himself. When he finished drying the last plate he set it on the rack and turned himself around, leaning on the counter and drying his hands with the towel on his shoulder.

"You've made yourself comfortable here." Liam mused, looking up at the older man.

"Yes, Chaeronea has been very kind. I'm just trying to help out where I can." He nodded. Liam nodded back, going back to his food, which he ate slowly. William considered this for a moment, going to sit down across from Liam. "When I lost Wallace, I went into a kind of daze. Nothing seemed real. Everything I had planned; the honeymoon, the house, the kids, it was all out the window. I stopped thinking about the years ahead, and instead I only saw the next hour, two hours. As cliche as it sounds Liam, and you're a writer, that's why I mention it," William took a deep breath, "I was alive, but I wasn't living."

Liam pushed his plate away, "What changed?"

William took a minute to think about Liam's question, "The war ended. Suddenly I wasn't in combat anymore. It was like, when I was in combat, that's all I had to think about. I only needed to focus on not getting killed at that moment. There was no time to grieve or wallow, and I think that's why so many of us went along with The House. It was a distraction, to be fighting with them. But once it ended, well, suddenly I had time on my hands. I was no longer fighting, I was patrolling, or teaching. I spent my nights in my bed not worrying about if the other side was going to invade, so my thoughts wandered to her, to Wallace. I couldn't sleep, I stopped eating, and eventually I stopped feeling." William met Liam's eyes. "I was going to kill myself, and I was convinced that I should have died at the wedding instead of Wallace, so I went to put on the uniform I had been wearing that day for the wedding. I had never touched it since I took it off two years earlier, and when I slipped it on, I felt around in the pockets. That's when I found a note from Wallace that she had slipped in there before the wedding."

"What did it say?" Liam whispered.

William shook his head, "To be honest, I have no idea. I ripped it up, convinced I had failed her. But then I really started to think about *her*, and I realized that this life I was living, it was not what Wallace would want for me. So I took off the uniform and I started acting differently, making the most of myself, helping where I could. That kind of thing."

Liam took a deep breath, "It's so hard William." He admitted.

William nodded, "I know. I know better than most people." He made eye contact with the younger boy, "And I'm here for you. We are all here for you, and I think you know that." Liam nodded, "But I think you also know that sitting in this house is not what Sylvia would want from you."

Liam's gaze fell to the table, "But how do I move on? I can't just leave her behind."

"You don't have to, at least not right now. All you need to do is take it one step at a time. Keep her in your heart as you do. Start by leaving this house. Write an article. Do something, anything. Just one step at a time, and maybe someday, with Sylvia in your heart, you'll find someone who understands, and who you can be with without forgetting her."

"Have you?" Liam asked.

William shook his head, "Not yet."

ooo

"Okay."

"Okay?"

Liam leaned on the doorway of Ryan's office. People moved in and out around him, gathering boxes of Clementine's old artwork and knickknacks and replacing them with more of Ryan's things. Some people painted the bright colored walls a light gray while others moved the furniture around. Ryan sat behind the desk, looking up over an open file at Liam.

Liam moved further into the office, out of the door, to let two younger men move a giant picture frame out. "Okay," he repeated, "I want the job."

Ryan's eyes went wide, but he pushed his surprise down and pushed his glasses up. "Well, that's the right decision."

"Wait." Liam interrupted, "I have a condition." Ryan gestured for Liam to sit down in a chair in front of the desk, "I want people to be able to grieve. It's what the people want, and it's a ridiculous rule in the first place. I want The House to value the human life."

"Alright."

Liam paused, raising an eyebrow, "Really?"

"Sure. It doesn't go against my beliefs. People's lives need to be remembered so we can remember their mistakes and learn from them." Ryan expressed.

Liam shook his head, rolling his eyes, "Whatever. Your reasons are your reasons, as long as it goes through, that's fine."

Ryan stood up as Liam began to leave "I'm excited to be working with you." He added in his monotone voice, holding out his hand.

Liam let out a small laugh, "This is going to be interesting." And he walked away, leaving Ryan's hand suspended over his desk.

ooo

Liam's hands were sweating as he grabbed the door knob to Chaeronea's house. The walk back to her house had given his anxiety enough time to fill his chest as he wondered whether or not he was making the right decision. His brain started to swim and he became dizzy. *Wow, today has been a day. I'm a mess,* he thought. He nervously smiled at the wooden door, realizing that this had been the first time he had been outside for weeks. Suddenly, the thought of going inside didn't seem so appealing.

Liam took a deep breath before opening the door and walking in. His feet seemed to glide into the apartment and he really didn't know how to describe how he was feeling. He was walking in without a plan, and suddenly a wave of vulnerability hit him.

Then he heard Chaeronea drop something and curse about some sort of stain. He smiled to himself, and he heard Sylvia's voice in the back of his head, telling him he had to let someone in.

Liam stood with his hand on the doorknob, on a door he had just closed, standing in the entryway of Chaeronea's house. He debated with himself and realized he should have thought this over sooner. He wanted to tell Chaeronea his news, but he didn't know how'd she react.

He was scared.

"Hello?" Chaeronea called from inside the house.

Liam realized that she had probably heard the door close, and that it had probably happened at least a minute ago. He had been standing there an unreasonable amount of time.

He put his keys down on the table in the hall, "Hey," He said as he rounded the corner, smiling a little.

Chaeronea was standing next to the couch folding a white blanket with a red stain in the middle, "Hey." She answered, and everything he was worried about suddenly did not seem so important.

Liam closed the space between them. Chaeronea fit inside his arm. Liam didn't know what brought them together, just that a hug felt really good at that moment.

And Liam knew that he would never have done this with Sylvia. He knew that he would have approached her differently. He would have started by helping her with folding the blanket. He would have folded it with her, slowly getting closer to her, until they were face to face. And then, he would have kissed her.

Liam knew that Chaeronea was not Sylvia. Liam knew they were different. Who was to say who was more broken? Who needed him the most? Who was to say one could be replaced with the other? They were two different people.

When Liam and Chaeronea broke apart, Liam kept his hands on her arms. "What was that about?" She asked shyly, smiling.

"I just," He breathed, "Needed it." Chaeronea nodded, Liam breathed out, "Chaeronea, I have to tell you something."

Chaeronea raised an eyebrow, "Oh?"

"Yeah. Maybe we should sit." Liam grabbed her hand as he sat on the couch, she followed him.

Liam took a deep breath, weighing his words, before finally saying, "When Ryan came to see me the other day, he offered me a job."

Chaeronea held his gaze for a second too long, "I know."

"What?"

Chaeronea blushed, "I heard, sorry. I didn't mean to eavesdrop, but well, I was nervous about having him here. So I listened in."

"Oh."

"Are you mad?" She asked.

"No," Liam responded immediately, "Of course not, you were protecting me. Thank you." He kept her gaze.

"Thank you." She whispered, "So, did you take the job? Is that where you went today?"

Liam nodded, "Yes. I know it sounds crazy, but I feel like I can do more on the inside than the outside. And Sylvia wouldn't want me to just sit around and wallow in my depression all day. I need to do something active, productive. Something helpful."

Chaeronea took his other hand, nodding, "I understand Liam. But can I ask, why now? Why not tell me before?"

"I don't know." He shrugged, "I think because I was so confused about it. But now, I just, I think it's time I start talking about it, you know? I want to talk about that confusion, and you're the one I want to talk to."

Chaeronea's smile grew, and Liam leaned in to hug her. Over her shoulder, Liam saw Sylvia standing in the corner. Her brown hair shiny next to the window. Her eyes were bright. Liam almost pulled away from Chaeronea, but Sylvia nodded her head. This was what she wanted for him; she wasn't mad, she was proud.

CHAPTER FIVE

"You okay?" Chaeronea asked him, holding a box in her hands.

"Mm, yeah."

"I don't believe you." She said gently.

Liam took a breath, "I just never thought I'd have to do this."

"We can take it slow. It doesn't all have to happen at once."

"No, it should. I think that will be easier."

"Okay."

"Just don't get rid of anything, okay?"

"Okay." Chaeronea told him, turning back to the spice shelf, carefully grabbing jars and placing them in the box. Liam scanned the shop and watched Matilda pack away the books and William take the plants off their pegs where they were hanging. Liam glanced around and grabbed a box, headed upstairs. He walked through the kitchen to their shared bedroom. He took in their bed by the windows and the quilt Sylvia had made laying on it. He touched the old Christmas lights he had found for her and hung around the room. He sat on her side of the bed and held her pillow.

After a few minutes, he went to open the closet, her closet, and grabbed a dark green sweater she had never worn.

"I *hated* that sweater." Sylvia spoke. Liam jumped, dropping the sweater and turning around to face her. "Oh my gosh! I'm so sorry, I forget I'm a ghost sometimes." She smiled at him, and he almost cracked a smile.

"It's not your fault," He told her, "I'm also a little on edge today," He admitted.

Sylvia nodded her head, "I know." She went to pick up the sweater, "I remember when Matilda made this for me. She worked so hard knitting it, so I felt like I had to wear it, but it was just so-"

"Itchy." Liam finished, smiling up at her; words passing through their eye contact, he didn't need to say more. After a minute, he turned back to the closet, grabbing a white T-shirt. "I always thought it was funny that you had so many clothes, but liked wearing mine better," he smiled at the ground.

Sylvia shrugged, smiling back, "Your's smelled better."

He nodded, continuing to go through her things, "I think you looked better in them anyways." He added after a minute.

Sylvia kept her gaze on the back of his head as he worked, "I'm proud of you, Lee."

Liam stopped working and felt the material of the blue soft flannel he was holding. "I remember the last time you wore this." He smiled, "Two months ago, when you decided to make me a cake for my birthday and caught this on fire." He laughed, fingering the burnt bottom of the shirt.

"Liam," Sylvia said softly, "Don't do this to yourself."

"Do what?" He breathed out, acting indifferent.

"Make yourself the bad guy." Sylvia told him, moving towards closer and holding his hands, "You made the right decision with the job, and with Chaeronea-"

"Nothing is happening with me and Chaeronea." He assured her, pushing her hair behind her ear and holding her face in his palm.

Sylvia's hand went up to hold his wrist, "Liam, listen to me. It's okay for you to move on. I'm dead, and Chaeronea is here. She has always been here, she understands what you've been through."

"I'm never going to forget you." He whispered, silent tears starting to fall despite his best intentions.

"I know." She told him, "I'm not saying you are. I'm saying what you're doing Lee, it's healthy, and I want you to be healthy."

Liam opened his mouth, but he didn't know what he wanted to say. He searched Sylvia's eyes for anger, but all he found were answers, reassurances. Before he could find his words, he heard someone clear their throat inches away.

Liam moved his head and saw Ryan standing in the doorway. Liam's eyes quickly darted to Sylvia, but she was gone, and he dropped his hand, wiping at his eyes with the other. "Can I help you?" He asked, turning his back on Ryan and shoving the flannel into his own messenger bag.

"I stopped at Chaeronea's house but no one was home. So I thought maybe you might be here."

"What a detective." Liam breathed out, continuing to fold clothes.

"Liam, please." Ryan started.

Liam put down the pair of leggings he was holding, "Well, since you asked so nicely," He said sarcastically, "What can I do for you?"

"I just came to tell you that there is a Board meeting tomorrow morning. It starts at 10."

"And I should be there?"

"Yes." Ryan stated.

Liam thought for a second, "Okay, I'll be there."

Ryan gave a short nod, "Good. I'll leave you to your work then." And he started to walk away.

"Ryan, wait." Liam called out. Ryan slowly started to turn, his eyes confused behind his glasses. He raised an eyebrow. "What was your dad like?" Liam blurted out.

Ryan's face crinkled, "I wouldn't know. I was told by my social worker that I was left on the steps of a church by my mother, who left a note with me explaining that my father had died in a car crash and she couldn't care for me on her own."

Liam let the shock settle before responding, "What did you do?"

"I stayed with a foster family, never got moved. I tried to be the perfect son. Killed myself in school, got into the top colleges in America, then the top law school."

"So, what happened?"

"Your mother told me she was pregnant."

Liam went completely numb, his heart seemed to slow and he heard the rhythmic beats in his ears. "W-what?" He didn't hear himself ask.

"I was on track for great things, things I had wanted my whole life, but she was ready to throw all those things away for a family. She wanted me to drop everything, and I couldn't do that; her decision affected everything."

Liam shook his head. "My mom was an amazing person."

"I'm not saying she wasn't," Ryan stated blankly, "I was in love with her." Liam's eyes widened, "So before you ask why I left, let me tell you. At that moment, I saw someone else controlling my life. It wouldn't have mattered who it was. Your mother, my mother. It wouldn't even have mattered if I loved her or not, what mattered is that her decision made me no longer in control, and that was a problem."

Liam made eye contact with his father, "Do you think you've changed at all since that day?"

Ryan kept eye contact, "Yes." He started, "I learned the value of someone's life."

And he left Liam standing there amongst Sylvia's clothes.

CHAPTER SIX

One of Ryan's assistants, a man who introduced himself as Noah, showed Liam to the conference room. Liam walked inside and scanned the few faces who were already seated. Ryan walked in seconds later behind him, "Glad you could make it." He told him.

Liam nodded, "Where do I sit?" He asked quietly.

Ryan led him to a chair to the right of the head, "Here," and Liam nodded again.

"Should we start everyone?" Ryan asked the group, and Liam watched people he didn't know nod their heads and take a seat around the long table.

He looked down to find a stack of papers in front of him, the first of which being an agenda. He scanned it quickly, finding his name next to the first item on the list. He glanced at Ryan, raising an eyebrow, but Ryan didn't return the look.

Ryan started the meeting, "Hello Board members. As you all know, this is our second meeting with me as The Chairman. Today, I would like to introduce you to my new business partner, Liam Wood."

Liam heard some small gasps around the table. "Wood?" Someone spoke, "Operations? What exactly will he be doing?"

Liam looked at Ryan, wondering the same thing. Ryan didn't blink, "He will continue his work as editor of the community paper, as well as starting a new project: the obituaries and birth announcements column of the paper." Liam's eyes widened, that was unheard of in The House.

Others thought so as well, "Obituaries? Birth announcements? What's that all about? We've never had those." A red haired woman with long curls and purple half moon glasses said.

Ryan sighed, "It's come to my attention that the community members want us to recognize life, and the value of it. It was actually Liam who brought this to my attention." He looked over at him, "Liam?" Ryan said, "Would you like to say anything about this?"

Liam's eyes widened at Ryan, but when he gave him an encouraging nod, Liam stood up, messing with the papers in front of him, "Board members, I believe what Ryan is trying to say is that we have taken into account what the people want-"

"When have we ever done that?" A black haired man interrupted, "Isn't Ryan's whole religion about how we aren't capable of making our own decisions? That's why we're here."

"John," Ryan spoke, "I suggest you don't interrupt Mr. Wood again," He turned back to Liam, "Go on."

"Board members, I think Ryan and I agree that Clementine ran things one way, and they didn't necessarily work. We think it's time to make some changes, and this is one of them. People need to be content with classification, right? So let's tell them that they matter, and that way they will be more open with the system because they will want to share with us; they will know we care."

"We all know what you're up to, Wood," John started again, "You're trying to reverse our community, all our hard work, and make it just like before the Awakening. I won't allow that."

"John." Ryan barked.

"No, it's fine." Liam waved off, "I understand how you feel, but I assure you that is not my intention. I'm just asking for this one thing, so that we can remember the people we've lost. So that if your significant other died, you can remember them, publicly mourn them." Liam answered, keeping eye contact with John.

Ryan looked around at the Board members, "I think that that's enough for today."

John shook his head, "Wood, I'm not letting this happen. Just because you lost the love of your life, doesn't mean we can change our morals. You should be put up for an act of declassication." And he walked out.

ooo

Liam walked into The House and made a beeline for his room. Chaeronea tried to make eye contact with him, "Hey how was the meeting?"

"Not right now." He told her, slamming the door behind him. He took a pillow off the bed, threw it across the room, and Sylvia caught it.

Liam did a double take. "Good catch." He choked out.

"I was a catcher for-"

"Five years in elementary school. I remember." He smiled.

Sylvia smiled, putting down the pillow. "Bad day?"

Liam ran a hand through his hair, "Horrible. These people, they're so messed up. And honestly, I am too."

"What do you mean?" Sylvia asked.

Liam ran his hands through his hair, "I'm working for the man who killed you Sylvia! That's messed up!"

"But he's also your father." Sylvia stressed, her voice soft.

Liam ignored her, "I'm working for the people who killed you."

"But you're working against them. You're on the inside making change." She tried.

"Then why does it feel so wrong?" Liam asked her.

"Survivors guilt?" She asked.

Liam nodded. "I just keep thinking, no matter what I do, it will never be enough. You still won't be here with me, well, like you were. Nothing is going to get you justice."

"I don't need justice." Sylvia sadly smiled, "I need you to be happy."

"I need you with me." He admitted, grabbing her hand, "They all said to give it time. I've tried to, and I know it's just been a few weeks, but the more time I give it, the more I realize you aren't coming back. I'm standing here talking to a ghost. I can't get over you, but I don't want to either. I'm just stuck here, desperately trying to stay in the past with you, and hopelessly trying to move on."

Sylvia gave a small smile, bowing her head, "Spoken like a true writer."

Liam noticed her sad smile, "Hey," He started, "I'm sorry. You know I love you being here, I just- it's so hard. It's so hard having half of you, having this ghost of you that no one else can see. It's like you just being here is this constant reminder that you *aren't.* I lose you every time I turn my back, and I'm so sick of losing you. I *love* you Sylvia Blue." Liam tilted his head up to get her attention.

"I love you too." She spoke softly and met his eyes, "But maybe it's time for you to really move on. Maybe it's time I go."

"No, V. I didn't mean it like that. This is just hard for me."

"No Lee, you're right. It's hard for you because I'm a constant reminder to the past." Sylvia lifted her gaze to Liam, who had silvery silent tears streaming down his cheeks, "You will never forget me, I know that. I know you love me, and you know I love you. But this isn't healthy anymore, it's not good for you. And I want what's best for you." She started to choke up. "I love you." She whispered.

Liam grabbed her face, "Don't go, please, I didn't mean it." He whispered. She leaned her forehead on his, "Don't leave. I love you Sylvia Blue. I love you."

But when Liam opened his eyes, she was gone.

○○○

He went to sit on the floor, up against the door, tears streaming down his face. "Chaeronea?" He whispered, "You there?"

Chaeronea curled her knees up to her chest against the door she had been leaning on, "I'm here." She told him through the wood.

○○○

"What's going on with you?" John Maverick, one of the most influential members of The House Board, stood on one side of Ryan's desk. His composure was calm, he took a deep breath, "This kid is changing you."

"I'm getting tired of this same old act, John." Ryan told the man, seething behind his glasses, "When we look back at history- and don't tell me it doesn't exist- what do we see? Famous people killing people. Clementine killing people, me killing people, and then on top of that, us failing to recognize when people have died in this world we've created. It's like we're right back to the genocides in Africa and Europe, or the government conspiracies in America, we're just trying to cover things up. Liam and I don't want to cover anything anymore, we want real change, we want to make a better world. One that keeps classification, one that tries their best to protect citizens from making bad decisions, but one that values life."

John sighed, "You can rant all you want Ryan, but the Board is planning on voting this down."

Ryan stood up, leaning against the desk and pointing his finger at the man across it, "I won't let them do that."

"This isn't a monarchy Ryan, you know that." John sighed. "The Board has the right to veto a proposal. Yes, your vote counts for more than ours, but in this case, you have the whole Board against you. We're united on this matter."

Ryan paced behind his desk, "I won't allow you to throw out Liam's plan. This is the right step for the community." Ryan's anger grew with each step.

"Look, Ryan. The kid's idea is good, but it's not realistic. We can't go changing fundamentals, that starts questioning, and we both know that's not good. This is what's happening, you better get on board."

Ryan started to protest when suddenly he started coughing, huge coughs that wracked his whole body, and pretty soon he was doubled over, hand to his mouth.

"Ryan, are you alright?" John asked, stepping towards Ryan who was doubled over his desk. Ryan waved him off, trying to stop the coughing, when suddenly he became dizzy.

He watched as the room spun around him. He felt pain in his chest and clutched at it, suddenly he was on the soft carpeted ground, the ceiling spinning above him. Then, there was John, peering over him. Ryan saw his mouth move but couldn't hear the words. He tried to tell John to stop spinning the room. Tried to tell him there were three of him, standing over him, but he couldn't.

And then Ryan saw black.

CHAPTER SEVEN

Liam was laughing for the first time in a while.

The four of them sat in Chaeronea's living room playing charades; Liam and Chaeronea against William and Matilda. They were just finishing William's turn where he had been tasked with acting out a baby goat. Liam had tears running down his face; happy tears.

"Okay! My turn. You ready Chaeronea?" Liam smiled at her, going for the bowl in the middle of the table. Chaeronea's smile grew, but before she could answer, there was a knock on their front door. Liam rolled his eyes, still smiling, "Wonder who that is." He got up to answer the door, Chaeronea following behind him.

Liam opened the door to a younger man Liam recognized but did not know the name of. He was Ryan's assistant, the one who had shown him to the board room. Nathan, maybe? Nick? It was on the tip of his tongue.

"Sir," The boy said, "You have to come quick. The Chairman is dying."

Chaeronea put her hand over her mouth.

And then Liam remembered - Noah- and he remembered when he and Sylvia had studied the meaning of names from an old book; it means rest, comfort.

ooo

Sylvia sat in front of the fire, "I love the fire. It's like a drama, waiting to see which log drops first." She said, completely seriously.

Liam grabbed her hand, "You're something else Sylvia Blue. I've learned so much from you."

"Oh yeah?" Sylvia smiled, leaning her head on his shoulder, "Like what?"

"That pancakes taste better with jam. That matching socks is ridiculous. That there are two sides to every story. That you can never stop falling in love."

ooo

The long gray curtains were drawn over the six windows in Ryan's room. The lamp next to his bed cast a golden glow on the side of his pale, sweating face. Someone had pulled a chair up for Liam, who was now sitting next to his father's four poster bed, but everyone had forgotten who had done it. The maroon carpet was dented by the weight of Chaeronea's shoes as she stood near the back of the room with some of the Board members and some of Ryan's closest acquaintances.

Ryan's house keeper brought a wet washcloth for Ryan's forehead and started to wipe away his white hair from his forehead, but Liam reached out for it. "Let me." He whispered, keeping his gaze on his dad. His fingers found its way around the cold cloth. The water matted Ryan's hair to the side of his head.

Ryan stirred with the contact of the cloth, opening his eyes to meet Liam's. He weakly pushed the cloth away, and he looked different without his glasses on, almost younger. He grasped Liam's hand with his own to try and sit up, using most of the energy he had left. "What the fuck happened?" Ryan struggled out.

Liam had to resist cracking a small smile, "I don't know." He admitted, "John said you passed out, you were clutching your chest."

Ryan opened and closed his mouth, it felt dry. The room spun ever so slightly and he closed his eyes for a few seconds to make it stop, "So, I'm dying then."

Liam looked down at the white old man, "Yeah, I think so."

Ryan nodded, his gaze going to the side, "I deserve it."

Liam shook his head. He had to fight his two sides of his brain. His mind told him, this is the man that killed Sylvia. His body ached, this is your father. "Don't say that." He struggled out, convincing himself, "Your life mattered to."

"You're right, it did. But that doesn't mean I don't deserve this. Liam-" He tried to continue, but coughs racked his whole body. Liam helped him sit up more. After a minute of coughing, he continued, "Liam, listen to me. This is important. You are Chairman now. They are going to try and take this away from you, but-"

"Me? *Chairman?*" Liam asked bewildered.

"Yes, you. Who else?" Ryan breathed out. Taking a deep breath, he went on, "This is how you make your change. Now *listen* to me, my resignation is in my desk drawer naming you as Chairman. It's been signed, just in case. You're going to have to work for this, they are going to try everything they can to stop you. Do what you have to, but don't give up."

"I don't know," Liam shook his head, "I can't be Chairman." He felt panic rise up his throat. He suddenly didn't want Ryan to die, and he couldn't tell if the feeling came from the shock of being named Chairman, or the fear of not knowing the man in front of him well enough.

"You can, and you will." Ryan told him, "Just listen," And he pulled Liam closer, "Don't be me, and don't fucking screw up." Liam started to protest, but Ryan had one more thing to say. His breath was heavy and his eyes were closed as he spoke, "I read through that paper you threw at me, and that Sylvia girl, she was a good catch."

And then, Liam had witnessed another death. Sylvia's had left him full of grief, Clementines had left him shocked, but this one left him numb. He realized once again how different death was then what a child perceived it to be. There was not an overaggrated last breath, there was no crying, and there was no final I love you.

Liam looked around the room of uncertainties; he thought about how hard it was to love someone who couldn't love you back. How hard it was to love someone you hated. How hard it was to get someone to love you.

He stared into his black and white world and wondered why wherever he went, people died.

He just wanted it to stop, and he didn't know why that was so hard. He didn't know why or how or when death had become the norm. He wondered who had wanted it that way. He wondered why they wanted it that way.

They couldn't keep living in black and white, humans were too imperfect for that, but they also couldn't live in a grey area, because it was too confusing for everyone.

But blue. Blue was the color of expression and life. Blue could make you feel sad or alive. It was wallowing depression and lively jazz. It was the color of rain and puddles that little kids stepped in, the horizon where the light sky connected to the deep blue sea. Blue was the denim in the jacket that fit perfectly, the color you saw on the last mountain in a landscape, the color of your childhood home.

The emotion that filled you when you finished a book. The happiness you felt when your favorite song was sung. The feeling you got when you saw the love of your life.

And Liam could see a perfect world that way.

It was wonderful.

It was blue.

END NOTE

Everyone has a blue in their life. For Liam, it was a person, the love of his life. For some, it's the color of their loved one's eyes, their favorite flannel, or the shade of the lake by their childhood home. It could be a fancy cheese or a type of music that makes you feel alive.

What's the blue in your life?

2021 Community Census

Name : Photo:	Jillian Sherwin 
Age:	18
Residence:	Rochester, VT
Occupation:	Senior in High School, Christian, Author of this book
Social:	Facebook: @AWorldColoredBlue Instagram: A_World_Colored_Blue
Likes:	-Being with friends -Listening to loud music in the car -Going to vintage stores
Dislikes:	-Yogurt -Country music (Excluding Taylor Swift's old albums) -Mice and rats
Sequel?	Maybe... :)

Made in the USA
Middletown, DE
22 May 2021

39868452R00195